SEX

DEGREES OF SEPARATION

A NOVELLA

BY

MAHOGANY STAR

For My M&M's

ACKNOWLEDGEMENTS

Thank you God, father for allowing me to write and for giving me the gift of discernment and determination, although I tend to procrastinate. To my husband Michael, thank you for everything, because there are too many things to name. To my mama Max thank you for believing in me and pushing me to move forward. To my two lifelines Michael-Jalen and Madison, I do it for you.

My sister Lateacha-Monique and niece Mikaylah, thank you both for your presence in my life. To my friends and family there's too many of you to name but I have to name a few. Luanda Colon-Smith, Nailaja Mingo, Taisha Rozier, Iasia McCord, Qtesha Carter, Lakeisha Porter, Shawnette Porter, Trina Porter, Cassandra Martin-Harris, Taisha Martin, Everlia Martin, Angel Colon, Yolanda Colon, Sonja Colon, Toni Colon, Maria Colon, Patricia Porter, Mary Porter, Ralphie Colon, Leon Addison, Ronald Graves, Shakina Punch, Connie Dobbin and Shamecka Williams thank you all for always supporting me. My grandmothers who are still with us, Ms. Mae Colon and Joyce Rozier, thank you both for loving me. I love you.

My friends who are like family and mean so much to me, Sadri Perkins, Nagina Phillips, Twanna Tolliver-Maheia, Kandece Francis, Tammy Hodge, Teri Williams thank you.

My cousin Ricky "Flav" Colon author of A Dangerous Love Affair, I'm so proud of you. I hope you continue doing what you are destined to do. To my editors Jamie Fleming-Dixon and Angelina Concepion thank you!

To anyone who has supported me from strangers to friends from school, to the people I grew up with. I want to give you my sincerest thanks.

It can be invasive to write at times. You're giving the reader your thoughts, may they be perverse or unpopular. You're giving people an inside to your mind and it can feel like you're being exposed, but at the same time there's nothing like telling a story. Nothing like getting some ideas out of your head and onto some paper. There's more to come and I hope you continue to read; this is just the beginning.

Always,
Mahogany Star

The Flesh Is Weak

Nina's Need

"FOR EVERY BEAUTIFUL WOMAN YOU SEE, I can show you a man that's tired of fucking her," said Jock, my husband of almost seven years, defending the notion of why he rationed the dick out to me only twice per week. Wednesdays and Fridays faithfully. My girlfriend, Shannon, rolled her eyes and joked, "Fuck you, Jock; I know Chaz will never get tired of fucking this right here."

"You damn right I won't as long as we can keep it freaky," Chaz agreed then stuck out his long thick tongue and moved it in a motion that could only mean one thing. I was in such a trance, watching his tongue thrash around, that I didn't feel my husband tapping me, asking if I was ready to leave.

We spent every Friday or Saturday evening with my husband's business partner, Chaz and his girlfriend, Shannon. We'd eat, drink and talk about politics until we drank enough liquor to talk about sex. Shannon and Chaz had only been together for two years, and she has a five-year-old daughter, Casey, from a previous relationship. She's a native of Frankfort, Kentucky, and Jock, Chaz and I went to college together in Kentucky. Jock is from

Lexington, Kentucky, while I was raised in New York and Chaz in New Jersey. Even with their different backgrounds, Jock and Chaz became friends their first year at the university. Jock was raised in a Southern home, with Southern- fried-fish-every-Friday values. Chaz, on the other hand, was born to an African-American teenaged mother and an Italian-American father, who was older, and they owned their neighborhood pizza shop.

Throughout their time in school, Jock and Chaz worked at local construction sites, and when they graduated, they decided to go into business for themselves with Robinson & Casone Construction. Jock and I started dating when he was a senior, and I was a sophomore. The weekend after I graduated, we were married in front of 200 guests on one of the largest golf courses in Kentucky. And because I received my degree in business management, we decided that I would work for the business so we could save money.

Shannon and Chaz had the sex life I wanted with my husband. Jock laid the pipe like no other until we said "I do." After that, he put me on a cock calendar, and I had to become satisfied with getting my back blown out only twice a week. Meanwhile, I had to sit and listen to Shannon tell tales of Chaz's legendary dick and how he put it on her every chance he got: "Girl, he fucked me on the stairs"; "Girl, we made love in the backyard under the stars"; "Nina girl, Chaz eats pussy like he's getting paid to do it."

This is what I hear, week after week. On the other hand, I can only share stories like, "Jock hit it from the back last night, and it felt so good!" I try to juice up my stories, but it never works, and Shannon looks at me with the "poor needy Nina look" she always gives me after I finish telling her how desperate I am to get fucked in the right way.

Lately, I had been so engrossed in planning our seventh wedding anniversary party, that I hadn't taken the time to reflect on if my marriage was even worth celebrating. For the most part, we had the marriage most women envied. Jock was a hardworking man who provided well for me. We enjoyed each other's company, and although I didn't feel we were making love like we should be, I had no reason to suspect he was cheating. I just felt myself become more and more sexually frustrated by the day. But as usual, I put my needs last and continued to believe that I should just be happy with the amount of dick he was giving me.

I looked at Jock as he drove and ranted about how Chaz is going to eventually get tired of Shannon's ass.

"He fucking that girl too much, and I tell you, next thing you know, Shannon is going to be telling you he cheating. I know my man, Chaz," Jock spouted. I sat there, watching his full, juicy lips move but no longer heard him. I was lost in the thought of Chaz's tongue whipping about under my skirt, and it was making me hot all over. I imagined his goatee covered in my love juices as he lifted me up on the dining room table and feasted on me like dessert.

"Nina, Nina? You listening to me?" Jock tapped my thigh.

"Yes honey, I'm listening. Ooh, it's Friday; can we get dirty tonight?" I asked.

"Dirty like how, Nina?" Jock asks like I'm a child.

"Just nasty! Let's get out the whip cream; let's get freaky; let's make a movie!" I lick my lips.

"You're joking, right? You don't want all that shit on our sheets. And a movie? Girl, what's gotten into you?"

"Nothing, Jock. Never mind, anyway. I must have eaten something bad because I feel an itch coming on," I mumbled to myself, oblivious to Jock's ongoing tirade.

I closed my eyes to completely tune him out and imagined what it would be like to have a night of spontaneous sex, like we used to. I thought to myself, *I'm feeling an itch all right, and it needs to be scratched. It's funny; it even has a name: the seven-year itch,* I thought.

◖◗

I awoke Saturday morning and began my usual routine, which consisted of picking up my five-year-old daughter, Allisa, from my mother-in-law's house, taking her to dance class and having a small breakfast with Shannon while the girls were there, dropping Allisa off back home for her "daddy time," going to the gym to play racquetball with Shannon, then returning home for family time with Jock and Allisa. It was all monotonous as every Saturday had been the same for the past year since Chaz and Shannon had begun dating.

I pinned my hair up, and stepped in the shower, still thinking about Jock's theory. I longed for the times when Jock would take a shower with me then make love to me with the hot water cascading over our bodies. Jock was so fucking gorgeous with the body of Adonis; women would stop and ask for his autograph, thinking he was the model Tyson Beckford. But Jock looked even better to me.

When I stepped out of the shower, I looked at myself in the floor-to-ceiling mirror. I was in pretty good shape for a 28-year-old mother of a five-year-old. I turned to look at my ass, which was still firm; my thighs were toned yet very womanly, and my hips, although nice, looked like they could hold a few more babies. My breasts weren't as perky as they were 10 years ago, but they looked good nonetheless. I stepped closer and looked to see if I could see any signs of aging around my eyes. I gently pinched my caramel skin to check the elasticity, then I blew myself a playful kiss before pulling my damp hair into a ponytail.

I threw on a pair of skinny jeans, a white tank top, and a pair of red ballerina flats. I glossed my lips since their plumpness used to turn Jock on all the time.

"Jock, baby I'm leaving! Call your mom and ask her to make sure Allisa's ready," I yelled into the backyard where Jock had already begun his weekend yard work.

"Okay, baby!" He yelled back. I paused to look at him. Even after being with him for nine years, I still got turned on by the sight of him. He was tall, dark and had a baldy. His muscular arms would put most men to shame, and he had a wide smile with a mustache that neatly covered his full lips and beautiful brown almond-shaped eyes. He was fine by all women's standards. I giggled to myself as I thought about my old nickname for him: my tall glass of chocolate milk.

When I got to my mother-in-law's house, Allisa came running out the door dressed in her leotard and a pair of sweatpants.

"Thanks for having her ready, Mama Fletcher," I called as I waved from the side of the car. I took in Allisa's appearance, proud of what Jock and I'd produced. Allisa was tall for her age; she could easily pass for seven. She has long, wavy hair like me but has her father's beautiful dark skin and his almond-shaped brown eyes.

"Hey Lissie, did you miss me?" I asked, bending down to kiss my baby.

"No, mommy. I just saw you yesterday morning before school." She smiled, showing that she'd lost one tooth at the bottom.

It was a hot Kentucky day, and as usual the dance school, was chaotic as some mothers ushered their daughters out of the class, while others, like me, rushed them into class. I saw Shannon's daughter, Casey, and immediately made my way over to the pretty little girl.

"Where's your momma?" I asked.

"She ain't feeling so good, so Chaz brought me," she said then looked over my shoulder. "Well, you better get in; class is starting, and Lissie's already inside," I told her.

I turned around and saw Chaz's fine ass walking towards me. He was deep bronze with a head of curly jet black hair that was cropped closely along the sides and tapered at the neck. Even though he wasn't my type, for some reason, when I looked at him lately, I would get all tingly.

"So Chaz, you on dance school duty this morning, huh? What's wrong with Shannon, and why didn't she call and tell me she wasn't coming? She knows we have our Saturday morning breakfast together, and I'm hungry."

"Shannon is hung the fuck over – one too many of my special Long Island Iced Teas. Plus, you know I put that ass to bed for real last night," Chaz replied, laughing. "But if you're hungry, I'll take you to get something to eat. I'll be your Shannon for the next hour." He walked to the door and held it open for me.

As I walked towards him, I couldn't help but notice his body through his wife beater. His bronzed biceps rippled with muscles. He had dark eyebrows and a nice nose with full lips. His eyes were dark, almost black, and they were so sexy and dreamy, almost making him look mysterious. We walked to a café down the block and took our seats.

"So what's my man up to this morning? Battling weeds or smoking some," Chaz asked, looking over the menu that the young Italian waiter had placed on our table.

"He's doing his usual, fighting the weeds, cutting the grass; you know, same shit, different Saturday," I answered then closed my menu since I decided on the French toast.

"What you getting woman?" Chaz asked.

"French toast with fruit. What about you?" I questioned.

"I'll have the same"

After we placed our orders and got our food, we ate and made small talk about work and the anniversary party I was planning. We finished our meal and started walking back to the dance school to wait for the girls to get out. I liked talking to Chaz I had so many questions for him but I didn't want to talk about much pertaining to Jock and myself. I changed the subject and asked him when he was going to marry Shannon.

"I've known you since college, and I think Shannon is the first woman I've seen you really get into. Look, you've even become a stepparent," I teased, playfully elbowing his arm.

"We'll see, Nina. I have to take my time," Chaz said then changed the subject. "So what you and boss man getting into for the rest of the day?"

"Well, I'm going to the gym to see if I can get in a match with someone else since Shannon is out of it. Then I'll go back home, cook, same shit I do every Saturday. What about you?"

"Well, I'm going to take Casey home, then probably ride my new bike to the gym and chill for the rest of the day. I don't really know; I live minute by minute." Chaz flashed me a smile.

"Oh that's right; you did get a new bike. I haven't ridden one in years, not since Allisa was born. And you know your friend won't go near one of those things."

"Yeah, I told my boy he tripping. Listen, since we're both going to the gym anyway, I'll give you a ride on the back of my new shit after your match.

I'll bring Shannon's helmet with me. It'll cool your ass off because I put some speed on that shit. If you think you can handle the ride, you're more than welcome," Chaz offered.

I hesitated for a moment, thinking about what Jock would say if he saw me on the back of Chaz's bike, or any bike for that matter.

"Sure, sounds really good. I'll meet you at the gym later; I'm looking forward to that ride." I said, letting my eyes linger a little too long on Chaz's lips.

I heard the chime noting that the class was over and the sounds of little feet as the door to the dance rooms came swinging open all at once. My thoughts were interrupted by the sound of my daughter's voice.

"Mommy I learned how to do a jetè today! It's was cool! Can Casey spend the night?" she rambled without taking a breath.

"I'll have to talk to your Dad; you know you have "daddy and me" time this afternoon. Shannon probably won't mind, but we'll see," I said, my mind totally somewhere else.

After I got home, I ransacked my walk-in closet, looking for my cutest racquetball outfit. I found my white tennis skirt and paired it with my white polo shirt that had the hot pink emblem. I pulled out my newest tennis shoes, and a hot pink sports bra and thong. I added some water and a little oil to my hair then brushed it into a slick, neat ponytail. When I came down the stairs with my gym bag on my arm, Jock's eyes lit up.

"Well damn, I can see your ass hanging out of that little skirt." He sounded annoyed.

"I'm going to the gym. You expect me to be covered in fabric from head to toe? Plus, this Kentucky heat is crazy. I mean, we get summer in New York, too, but this shit is crazy!" I exclaimed, trying to make an excuse for why I was going out the house damn near naked. I walked over and kissed Jock on the lips, and he slapped my ass as I went out the door.

I ended up playing Misty Stein in two matches before I saw Chaz walk onto the racquetball court. He wore black gym shorts and a black tank top with black tennis shoes. He exuded sexy without even trying.

"You ready to ride?" he asked.

"I sure as hell am!" I said then turned and bowed to Misty, letting her know I conceded the game. Chaz and I walked outside to leave.

"You better not get me hurt on this bike!" I teased as I mounted the seat behind him. He took off fast, giving me a burst of adrenaline. We rode fast down Main Street, and I could feel my little skirt blowing in the wind, exposing my ass and my hot pink thong to the world. As we rode, I noticed how good Chaz's body felt. I wrapped my arms around his waist more tightly, and I felt how hard his stomach was. When the bike revved up at every light, we'd take off again, and the bump from our take off would cause my clit to hit the seat with a force that made me hot. I knew Chaz could feel my hard nipples pressed against his back. We rode for 15 minutes or so, and it felt so good. When he pulled back up at the gym, I knew the throbbing between my legs needed to be soothed; I just didn't know by whom.

"I'm about to take my ass to the sauna; it's usually pretty empty around this time of the day. I can sit back, relax, and just think," Chaz told me as we walked towards the gym door.

"You mind if I join you? I always finish my time here at the sauna," I said nervously.

"No, the company would be good. I'm going to rinse off in the shower first, then I'll meet you in there."

I hurried to the locker room, undressed, and jumped in the shower. When I finished, I grabbed a towel and went to the sauna, hoping it wasn't too crowded. Just my luck, it was empty. As I sat down, Chaz walked in with a towel around his waist. His chest glistened from the shower he'd just taken; I wanted to drink the water dripping from it.

I watched him come in, and could instantly feel myself moisten.

"Yeah this is how I like it: empty," Chaz said as he took a seat near me. As far as I was concerned, he was still too far away, so I moved closer and began massaging his shoulders.

"Damn, Nina; you good with your hands. Jock's a lucky man," Chaz said, enjoying my massage.

"Well, he doesn't act like he knows he lucky." Chaz's skin was moist and hot in my hands, and he was so tight. I stood up behind him to get a better grip on the muscles I was massaging. Right when I stood up, my towel dropped. My instinct was to pick it up, but the throbbing between my legs wouldn't allow me. So I stood there with my nipples touching the back of his head, and my pussy rubbing against his back. Without saying a word, Chaz turned around and started sucking my waiting breast. He took the tongue I'd been waiting to feel, and caressed my nipple. Then, he took one hand and placed it on my pussy; my juices covered his fingers. When he massaged my clit, I quivered.

He gripped my ass with his other hand as he finger fucked me frantically. Standing up, Chaz stuck his tongue deeply into my mouth; he had a breast in each hand that he massaged intensely. I was lost in his kiss when he suddenly dropped to his knees and lifted one of my legs onto the sauna bench. He slowly licked my clit and sucked it gently. Then he dug his tongue in deep, sucking and licking. This was pure euphoria. My head was thrown back, and I was enjoying the pleasure when he lifted and gently pinned me against the wall, I wrapped my legs around his waist. We were against the wall near the sauna's door; he lifted me up and positioned me on his dick. I could've screamed at the entry; it was massive in length and width. My walls gripped his shaft tightly as he grinded in circular motions, in and out. Chaz put in work, and we were both hot and sweaty from both the steam of the sauna and the heat between us. He lifted me like I was light as a feather as he pumped in and out. I could feel myself about to cum, and I moaned out loud without even considering the fact that someone might hear me. As my juices poured all over him, he took out his dick and unloaded all over my stomach. He panted while he gently put me back on the floor. My feet were now back on the ground, and I quickly came down from cloud nine.

I grabbed my towel, suddenly remembering I was naked. Chaz picked his up, wrapped it around his waist and said, "Thanks for the workout, Nina. That was some good shit." He pecked me on the forehead then walked out. I sat there feeling a mixture of satisfaction and guilt. I ultimately threw out the guilty feelings and decided that I needed another dose of Chaz; with him, satisfaction was guaranteed.

《❀》

I tossed and turned all night long; trying rid my thoughts of the mind-blowing orgasm I'd received from Chaz. It was like he'd given me an early anniversary gift; I was now lying in bed, feeling a sexy that I hadn't felt in years. I smiled at Jock, who was sleeping so peacefully like he was dreaming sweet dreams. Meanwhile, I was daydreaming, smiling like a Cheshire cat.

Monday morning came fast, as it always does, and we were back at work. I wondered if it would be awkward for Chaz to see me after what had happened. As if my thoughts were being played out, he walked into my office.

"Morning, Nina. I'm going to get me and Jock some coffee; you want some?" He asked as casually as he's always done.

"Uh no, no thanks; I have some already," I managed to stammer.

"Alright then; tell J-money I'll be right back if he asks for me."

I sat back in my chair, and my thoughts drifted to what it would be like to fuck Chaz on my desk. Me, laid out, spread eagle and him licking and sucking every inch of me. Or even better, me lying across my desk as he stood naked in front of me, pounding me with my legs on his shoulders. I felt myself moistening when my husband walked into my office.

"Nina, Nina, snap out of whatever deep thought you're in. I need that report for the Westman project done by Friday afternoon," he snapped. "Okay, honey?" He added to soften the demand.

"No problem, baby. Listen; come here," I told him, leaning forward in my chair.

"Yeah baby, what is it? You know we got three sites to visit today."

"Why don't you close the door, and let me swallow you real quick?" I offered in a sultry tone.

"Listen baby, that sounds good, but while you're swallowing me, time will be ticking away. And there is too much work to be done around here for that kind of play.

"By the way, did you make the flight arrangements for Chaz's trip to New York? There's a lot of money to be made up there with all the reconstruction they're doing in the boroughs. Chaz needs to put our bid in before they close it." Jock said, changing the subject.

"Yes, I made his arrangements."

"And my family is supposed to arrive on Thursday; did you check with your mom and let her know that my aunt and cousin would be staying with her until my family leaves Sunday morning?" I asked, annoyed that he always found a reason to blow me off.

"Yes, of course. And I knew I could count on you to stay on top of things here," he replied then walked out of my office.

Monday seemed to drag on; Tuesday was like a day that would never end. I needed Wednesday to come so I could feel Jock inside of me, and perhaps I could stop thinking about the way Chaz felt.

After putting Allisa to bed, I put some satin sheets on the bed, and jumped in the shower. I waited an hour for Jock to come to bed before I headed down to our study to find him asleep.

"Jock wake up!" I yelled, shaking his shoulder.

"Oh! Sorry, babe. You know I put in some work with the grunts today at the Connor Subdivision. Got a brother feeling like an old ass man." Jock muttered groggily.

"Well, I got something to make you feel like a young ass man," I told him as I stood in front of him then turned around and bent over.

"Damn, Nina; you look good as hell. But tonight you got to do all the work. I'm lazy as shit right now." Jock stood and stretched his arms, yawning.

I sighed, realizing my fantasy wasn't coming true tonight. I ushered Jock up to the shower and into the bed. I sucked his dick for a few minutes before sitting on it and fucking him to sleep. He came in a matter of minutes, and I was left to play with my clit, engrossed in the memory of Chaz banging me against the wall in the steam room. That night, I decided I needed to create a few more memories before I left Chaz and his fantastic dick alone.

∙❧❧∙

Thursday, I walked in the office looking cuter than usual. I had on a black pencil skirt, a white, sleeveless blouse with ruffles on the front, and a pair of patent leather red pumps. I'd slicked my hair back in a chignon and applied a nice copper red lipstick. When Jock and I arrived at the office, Chaz was already there, and I was surprised to see Shannon in his office when we arrived. I hadn't talked to her since Saturday when I checked on her.

"Well, good morning to you too, miss," Shannon greeted with a smile on her face.

"Hey girlie, how you be?" I asked, jokingly.

"I'm good. I just decided to stop in after I dropped Casey off at school. Isn't your family arriving today for Saturday?"

"Yes, I pick up my mother and aunt tonight."

"Okay, well, I'll call you later so we can catch up."

"Okay baby girl," I told her, catching Chaz eyeing my ass. I couldn't help but smile to myself.

Throughout the morning, I would walk past Chaz and Jock, switching and bending over conveniently. Chaz would look hungrily, but Jock paid me no attention. When Jock left for a client meeting that was a few towns away, I sat in my office, trying to think of a way I could get a few moments alone with Chaz. I paced the floor until I couldn't take it anymore. I headed out and told Rosa, our receptionist, I was running out for coffee and would be back soon. I knew Chaz was outside, using a crane to move some cinder blocks from around the business. I carefully stepped around the rocks in my pretty pumps and looked around to make sure no one would see me. I thought I would break my ankles trying to walk in four inches heels on rocks and gravel. As soon as I came into his line of vision, we locked eyes, and without words, he extended his hand and I stepped in. Since the window to the crane only exposed him from the chest up, I knew it would be a great opportunity to taste him.

Without words, I hiked my tight skirt up around my waist and knelt in front of him. When I unzipped his pants, I saw that his dick was already brick hard and standing at attention. I grabbed a hold of it as if I were gripping a pole and placed as much of him as I could into my mouth. I sucked him wildly, taking time to swirl my wet tongue on the head of his penis. His dick was like chocolate, and his pre-cum was semi-sweet. I used one hand to play with his balls, which grew tighter by the second, and I used my other hand to stroke it, while my mouth moved up and down his shaft. My saliva dripped from the sides of my mouth onto my hands as he slowly moved in and out of my mouth. I could feel his arms above my head, still operating the large machine. My panties were soaking wet. Just when I felt he was about to blast, I heard a voice.

"C, have you seen Nina? I hope she finished the expense report for the Westman job. I have to meet them tomorrow with the final numbers," Jock yelled.

"Nah man, I haven't. She probably went out for lunch or something," Chaz managed to say. I was motionless, but I kept his hardness in my mouth.

"Man, you sweating up in that motherfucker. Let me find out we need to get air conditioners for those shits," Jock joked.

"Nah, J-money; I been eating too much salt. Think my pressure up," Chaz humored him.

"Damn, negro! You sounding like an old ass man and yo' ass just making 30."

"Fuck you, J; move yo' ass out the way so I can get this shit moved before I leave."

"Aright, man. I'm taking my black ass inside where the air conditioner is on full blast!" Jock walked away, chuckling.

I got back to what I was doing, using deep, long strokes, knowing it was about to come to an end. I sucked faster, stroking faster while I tried to take as much of his dick as my mouth and throat would allow. Without a sound, he shot a warm, hefty load in my mouth, and I savored every drop. Although he was silent, his body shook like he'd been hit with a little electrical shock.

I looked up and saw a big grin on his face. He looked around like a private eye then said, "Alright Ni; the coast is clear. You better get in there before he comes back out looking for your sweet ass."

I winked at him, and without a word, stepped out of the crane, straightened my skirt, and walked back into the office.

"Mr. Robinson was looking for you," Rosa said without turning from her screen.

"Thanks, Rosa."

I walked into Jock's office to find him ending a call. He waved me in before hanging up.

"Where were you, baby?" Jock asked.

"Oh, I made a quick run out for a doughnut; I wanted to eat light today."

"Well, you should've picked something less messy than a doughnut. You still have some frosting on the side of your mouth. Next time, eat a salad," Jock teased, I thought I would faint, but that didn't stop me from using my tongue to lick the sides of my mouth, hoping to taste a little more of Chaz.

"Let me go email you the expense report before I forget," I told him before making my way out of his office.

Later that evening, I picked up my mother and aunt from the airport, and it felt so good to see them. I hadn't been home to Harlem in almost a year, and this was the first time my mother had been down in two years.

"Look at my princess!" My mother screamed as she embraced me tightly. Even though she was middle aged, you could tell my mother is a native New Yorker by her looks: her hair was pinned up in a Dubi courtesy of the neighborhood Dominican salon; her tips were long with a classic French manicure; and she wore a two-piece linen short set with brown leather sandals, showing her manicured toes. My aunt was dressed similarly, and for some reason, she still wore a gold cap on her side tooth.

I dropped my aunt off at my mother-in-law's house, which was glad for the company.

After getting my mother settled in at my house, I called Shannon, and we made a date to meet for lunch the next day.

When I saw Shannon walk towards our usual table at the Mexican restaurant we always went to, I felt a little bad for what I was doing with Chaz. But it wasn't like I wanted to take Chaz away from her; I just wanted to borrow his dick from time to time. That shit was so good; he should sell it on eBay to the highest bidder. Shannon and I embraced when she got to the table, and after we ordered, we began our gabfest.

"Girl, you looking good these days. You're glowing! Jock must finally be laying the pipe right!" Shannon joked.

"He always lays it right, just not enough. But I'm working on it. We are going to recapture our passion one way or the other," I told her., *I'm going to recapture it with or without him,* I thought.

"So, what's up with you and brother-man? Everything good?" I questioned.

"Oh yes; everything is great! Chaz is so good to me and Casey; I'm really feeling him." She grinned.

I was relieved to hear that nothing had changed in their household. "Chaz is a good man, and I'm so happy for you guys.

"Hopefully, he won't get distracted like his buddy and start penciling your ass in for lovemaking like it's a meeting or some shit. I tell you, I'm surprised Rosa hasn't started sending me meeting requests through Outlook just to schedule our lovemaking!" I teased, but I was really serious.

"Girl, I don't know what I would do if Chaz started being stingy with his shit. Girl, he got me so used to that good shit, I know I'm dick whipped. In all honesty, I don't know if I've ever had it that well, and believe me, I've had my share of dick."

We both laughed, but I couldn't help but think, *Girl, didn't your mama ever tell you to keep how good your man is in bed to yourself?*

I saw the excitement in Shannon's eyes as she talked about Chaz, and I understood the feeling he gave her. They really made a cute couple. Shannon had pretty, clear dark skin, long black hair and one of those Southern asses with the small waist and bubble butt that made you wonder what they add to the grits.

She was a good person but made the mistake of messing with a married man, who told her he would leave his wife but never did. Fortunately for her, his wife accepted Casey as her husband's child and is really good to her.

"So what are you going to do when Chaz leaves for New York on Sunday? Have you thought about going with him?"

"I thought about it, but I know he won't be coming back until next Saturday, and I don't want to leave Casey for that long."

"I know the feeling. I wouldn't want to be away from Lissie that long either. But there's a lot of ass in my hometown, so don't let Chaz get a whiff, and leave your ass down here!" I warned, only half joking.

"I tell you one thing, he can go up there and fuck around and move if he wants, too, but the dick and the tongue stays with me!"

I laughed with Shannon, knowing the power that lay between that man's legs.

"Are you taking Casey to the fair tomorrow after dance class, or are you just going to get ready for the party?" I asked, changing the subject.

"Yeah, we're going to go home, get changed, then stroll the fair for a little while. I have to get my hair done, so we won't be there that long. I know you guys are going."

"Yes, Jock promised Allisa he would take her. I was thinking about staying home and just getting myself beautified while they're gone, but I'll probably come too if Jock promises we won't stay too long."

"Okay, so, whose house are we at tonight?" Shannon asked.

"I think it'll be yours, since my mother's at my house. And I have an in-house sitter tonight, since my mother can't get enough of Lissie."

"Okay, I should be there around nine, after I drop my stuff off. I'll order Caribbean."

"Sounds good," I replied, scooping up the last of the yellow rice on my plate.

❦

It was a hot, sunny, and sticky Kentucky day. The fair was noisy and chaotic with kids oohing and ahhing at the sights of the caged animals and screaming on the rides. After taking Allisa on a few rides, we bumped into Shannon, Chaz and Casey.

"I'm surprised your ass could get up this morning," Jock told Chaz, giving him a pound.

"Yeah, man. I slept 'til 12 this afternoon. I was hungover like a motherfucker."

"I hear you. I kept my ass in the bed until Nina got back from taking Lissie to dance. No yard work for me today. Where ya heading to next?" Jock asked.

"We're about to take Casey on the merry-go-round," Shannon stated.

"Oh, okay. Well, we're taking Miss Allisa for some cotton candy, then we're going to take her to look at some of the animals before heading home," I told them, looking at Chaz. I think he could see the look in my eyes that said I needed him, but there was nothing he could do about it since we were at a crowded fair in the middle of the day.

As soon as we got Allisa her cotton candy, she decided she wanted to go on a few more rides. I told Jock that I would hold her treat and walk around to find some funnel cake. I walked until I spotted Chaz and Shannon; I stood behind the ticket booth for the Big Wheel. I stayed out of Shannon's line of view, but once I caught Chaz's eye, I discreetly motioned for him to follow me. He said something to Shannon then started towards me. I walked a few feet ahead of him in search of a quiet place; I only needed whatever few minutes he could give me. Finally, I found a large steel cage with a brown drape away from anyone's view. I could smell that it housed some kind of animal, but I didn't care as long as it would give me a moment of privacy.

As soon as I stepped beside it, Chaz walked up and gently grabbed the back of my neck and lay a hot, deep, wet tongue-thrashing kiss on me. I immediately dropped to my knees as he unbuckled his pants. I was eager to taste him again. Just then, I remembered I was still holding my daughter's cotton candy, so I pinched off a large piece of it and put it in my mouth along with his dick. The sweetness from the cotton candy made his dick that much more delectable. Right when his pre-cum hit my tongue, he removed himself from my mouth, grabbed me by the shoulders, and bent me over. My yellow sundress flew up around my shoulders, providing me with a small breeze. Before I knew it, he'd grabbed a handful of cotton candy, slid my black thong to the side, and placed it between my ass cheeks. Bending me over even more, he commenced to licking me from the front to back. I was so enthralled in the feeling that I held onto a bars of the cage. Without warning, he put his dick in me with one hard thrust. I moaned loudly, so he put his hand over my mouth and pounded deeply in and out of me. Waves of pleasure washed over me, and I could feel myself dripping lust juices as my leg shook from my orgasm. As he sloshed in and out of me, I heard growling and realized that we must've been near the lion's cages. Chaz's pace picked up, then he came all over my ass. I stood up, out of breath, but quickly gained my composure. I hurriedly pulled down my sundress and rushed away without a word, leaving Chaz panting and the lions growling. I blended back into the crowd and soon saw my daughter sitting on her daddy's shoulders as they waited in line for the mini roller coaster.

"Hey, guys; there you are! Jock, we have to be leaving soon. I have an appointment to get my hair done," I said.

"Mommy, where's my cotton candy?" Allisa demanded.

"Oh, honey. Sorry, mommy got hungry and ate it. But when you finish the ride, we'll get you some more."

After I told her that, I couldn't help but think that it was the best cotton candy I'd ever tasted.

⋘◎◉⋙

The time had come for my seventh wedding anniversary party. Our friends and family were already gathered at the hall, waiting for Jock and I to arrive. Shannon and Chaz

My dress for tonight was custom-made; it was a cream-colored strapless dress made out of chiffon silk. Pearls lined the trim at the top and bottom of the dress, and it fit me like a glove. My hair was blown straight with a slight curl at the end, and it cascaded just below my shoulders.

As I stood in the bathroom mirror, applying my mascara, Jock came in and stood behind me, staring at me through the mirror. He looked so gorgeous in his cream tux, and it complimented his chocolate skin very well.

"Jock, why are you staring at me?" I asked, trying not to sound nervous as I applied the last of my makeup. Without answering, Jock moved closer and moved my hair away from my neck.

"Nina, you are the most beautiful, perfect wife and mother. I love you." He pulled out a beautiful pearl necklace and placed it around my neck. It was so beautiful it took my breath away. I turned around and lay a deep kiss on Jock. The sight and scent of him made me hot, and I felt the bulge in his pants growing as it pressed against me. I started unbuttoning his pants, but he stopped me.

"Nina, we have 75 of our nearest and dearest waiting for us at this hall. We can pick this up later," he said as he gently removed my hand.

"Okay." It was all I could say, so I turned around and reapplied the lipstick I'd just lost to Jock's lips.

When we arrived at the hall, the DJ cued, "Anniversary" by Tony! Toni! Toné! As we entered. Everyone cheered as we walked hand-in-hand with smiles. I was truly happy, and I loved being Mrs. Robinson. Any woman would. But as happy as I was, I couldn't help but notice Chaz raising his champagne glass to us and nodding his head in approval, while we made our way to the dance floor.

His black tuxedo made him stand out from everybody else in the room, or maybe it was just him. It fit nicely, showing off his broad shoulders and back. His goatee looked so neat, and his hair was freshly cut. Shannon looked gorgeous, too, in a gold strapless dress that showed her long, toned legs.

I looked around and saw the kids running around, playing and enjoying themselves, and our families were mingling with each other.

Jock and I made small talk with everyone who came our way with gifts and congratulations on our marriage. We stopped for a minute to laugh with Shannon and Chaz about the older folks on the dance floor still getting their groove on. After my fifth or so glass of champagne, I needed some air. I started to just step outside of the hall but thought against it, because I knew there would be a crowd of smokers out there, ready to make small talk. And I was all talked out for the night.

My thoughts drifted to the original tour of the hall, and I remembered the owner taking me to the roof and showing me that some people had rooftop parties when the weather wasn't too humid. So, I decided to I make my way to the roof.

When I got there, I was surprised by the nice breeze. "Well, why the hell didn't I have the party up here?" I thought out loud. I ran my fingers along the cool decorative silver metal piping that ran along the outskirts of the roof and took in the environment. I could see all the lights from the small city.

I jumped when I felt the warmth of a hand touch my back. Almost instantly, I recognized the touch, but I wouldn't or couldn't turn around for fear of what I might do. I knew he'd been watching me the entire night, and in the back of my mind, I think I was hoping he would follow me up here to put out the fire Jock had started earlier that evening.

I felt the zipper of my dress being pulled down slowly. I silently prayed to myself that it was Jock, but I knew his touch. Once my dress was fully unzipped, I felt his lips on my shoulders. I was standing there on the roof, in my cream-colored, pearl-covered Chanel pumps, with my dress around my ankles, my ass out, and a room filled with my family, friends – not to mention my husband – right below me. In spite of all that, I couldn't stop myself at that point, even if I wanted to.

The champagne had me feeling lightheaded, and his touch had my body feeling free. As he kissed my shoulders and neck, I threw my head back to give him access to my mouth. He pushed his tongue in deeply, taking the time to suck on my bottom lip. I still had a shred of hope that it was Jock behind me. But when he slid my thong to the side and slid himself into my puddle, all hope was lost.

He was pressed against my back, so close we were almost one, as he pumped in and out at a slow pace. A moan escaped my lips when he picked up the pace. I could feel my juices dripping as he brought his head to my back. We came simultaneously with him panting and roaring in my ear while gently nibbling on it.

He pulled himself out of me then quickly picked up my dress and zipped it up. I still hadn't faced him, but when I turned around; I saw the door to the rooftop close. I felt a little dizzy as I made my way to the stairs, and I wasn't sure if it was from the orgasm, the alcohol, or both.

Sunday came, and I woke up with my period. Shamefully, I was relieved to see my family go and that Chaz was leaving for New York with them that day. I was glad because I figured it was the perfect week for him to be gone since I wouldn't be able to do anything with him anyway.

Every day that he was gone, I thought about that dick. I soothed myself by sucking Jock's cock on Wednesday, and by Friday, my period was gone, and I was all too ready to feel his hard dick inside of me.

When Jock came to bed that Friday night, I had porn playing on the flat screen in our bedroom. I lay naked with my legs draped over our foot post, while I masturbated to the threesome going on in the movie. Jock was instantly aroused but didn't say a word. He just climbed on to me and engaged me in a 69, which I was all too happy to partake in. It'd been so long since we'd done it, and it felt amazing. After Jock finished eating me, he flipped me over and put it in. I gasped at the feeling. He pumped for about 10 minutes or so before he unloaded in me. I always enjoyed sex with Jock; I just wanted it more often.

It was the day of Chaz's return, and the rain poured all day long. But on the sunny side, he would finally be back. Shannon seemed really excited when she called me.

"Girl, I've got to take Casey to Frankfort to see her dad. I forgot, and I won't be back in time to pick Chaz up."

"Oh, okay. Well, I'll just ask Jock to go get him. I'm sure he won't have a problem picking his boy up," I told her.

We hung up, and I went right to Jock to deliver the message because I knew Chaz's plane was supposed land at nine tonight.

"Jock, honey, Shannon just called, and she's not going to be able to pick Chaz up from the airport. Can you do it?" I inquired.

"Damn, why can't she?" Jock asked in an annoyed tone.

"She has to take Casey to Frankfort," I explained.

"Well, I just talked to my mother, and she needs me to come over and fix a few things around her house. Plus, the roof is leaking, and you see all this rain. I'm not leaving here for at least another hour, and you know when I get over there, there's no telling when I'm going to leave. You know she's always got stuff lined up for me to do."

I knew that was true. Jock had his work cut out for him at his mama's house.

"Hey, why don't you pick Chaz up? I can take Allisa with me," Jock suggested.

"Oh, Jock... Do I have to?" I asked like I really didn't want to.

"He went on a trip for our business, so I'd say yeah!" He teased.

"Well, since you put it that way..."

I was about to walk away when I heard Jock say, "Oh, and, by the way, Nina, you tasted so good the other night. You've been looking real tempting lately. Girl, you keep it up, and you may make me get off my schedule."

I just smirked then turned to go upstairs, thinking how I would welcome Chaz back to Kentucky.

After Jock and Allisa left, I jumped in the shower. I trimmed my pussy, washed my hair, and decided to air dry it. I fingered a little moisturizer through it and decided to let the curls be free. Then, I applied my sensual body lotion and matching body spray. I looked at my naked body in the mirror, trying to figure out what I was wearing, but I ultimately decided I'd greet him in nothing but my new black Manolo Blahnik® pumps. I pulled out a sweat suit to throw in the car for after we were done then put on my Burberry® trench coat and headed out the door.

After I pulled into the parking lot at the airport, I applied my gloss and waited for him to come out. He spotted my black Benz and smiled. As he loaded his bags into the trunk, I stepped out and walked to the passenger's side, opening my coat just enough that he could see I was nude. I sat in the passenger seat, and as if on cue, he got in on the driver's seat. When he sat down, I could see his dick pressing against his jeans, begging to be released. I quickly unbuttoned his pants and began devouring him.

"My nasty nymph Nina," he moaned, guiding my head up and down, caressing my wet hair. Within minutes, he came in my mouth; I sat up and saw people rushing to their cars, remembering that we hadn't left the parking lot. My phone started ringing, and I saw it was Jock; I just couldn't answer at the moment.

We left and rode in a comfortable silence. There was no need for words since we both knew what I was there for. When I noticed him pulling into our office parking lot, I knew he was eager to give me what I needed. He unlocked the dark, quiet office, and I walked ahead of him, towards my office. Once we stepped inside, he pulled me close then put his tongue in my mouth. He moved to my neck as he opened my coat and let it drop to the floor. We backed up to my desk, and with the exception of my monitor, he swiped my desk clean. He lay me on the desk, kissing me all over then stopped at my breast and sucked each one like they nourished him He then inserted two fingers, moving them in and out as he simultaneously played with my clit. I moaned and panted, trying to catch my breath; I felt amazing. He kissed his way up to my stomach and back down, sticking his tongue in my hole. He swirled his tongue around my clit, licking it, applying heavy then light pressure. I grabbed his hair, working his head between my legs. I didn't realize I had his head locked between my legs until he tried to come up for air.

He stood up and placed his log inside of me. I inhaled deeply so I could take him all in. He lifted my legs around his waist and grinded in slowly at first. Then he sped up and went hard and deep. My walls tingled as he pumped in and out of me in a circular motion, making sure I was pleased. I had squeezed my eyes shut, enjoying the feeling when he flipped me over. He then put it in my wet spot and started banging away. I was so deep in the feeling and in the moment that I almost screamed when he put a finger in my ass. It caught me by surprise, but after the initial shock, it felt good as he moved it in and out to the same rhythm of his dick. Before I knew it, I was throwing it back at him, begging him to go deeper and harder. When I came, I collapsed, face forward, on my desk. A few seconds later, Chaz pulled out and stood over my face while jerking his dick off.

I was satiated after getting my fix, but suddenly, the realization of what we'd done and where we did it started to kick in. I grabbed my trench and put it on. After Chaz pulled his pants up and buttoned them, we locked the office. We didn't say a word on the way to his place. He was visibly worn; I knew that since I drained him, he would be of no use to Shannon tonight. I just hope I could get home and showered before Jock got in.

I breathed a sigh of relief when I pulled up and didn't see Jock's Range wasn't in the driveway. I hopped in the shower to wash Chaz's cum out of my hair then went to bed because I was exhausted from my workout.

⟪◉ ◎⟫

When I returned to work the next day, I walked into my office and hurriedly closed the door behind me before Jock caught a glimpse of the papers strewn about. A smile crept onto my face when I thought about how the mess was made.

My mind wandered, and I thought about how Jock had been complimenting me more and more lately and it felt well. He'd been telling me it was the glow of my face that turned him on.

And later that week, he went off his schedule, and we actually had sex on Tuesday *and* Wednesday.

Lately, I'd been feeling so sexy, and when I had the house to myself, I'd put on a pair of sexy, four-inch heels, my long pearls, and lots of baby oil and. I'd blast "Sexy Love" by Neo or whatever song that described my mood at the time and dance around my bedroom naked and erotically like a stripper.

Today, when I was in my sexy routine, I felt a touch from behind and jumped. When I felt the sensuality of his hands, all my tension melted away. I didn't hear Jock come in, but he must've been watching me for a few minutes.

Jock slowly traced my body with one of his hand, like he was marveling at a statue. He turned me around to face him then caressed my breast gently before placing one in his mouth. His tongue circled my nipple as he squeezed my ass. He then kissed me on the mouth then moved to my neck. A few minutes later, he made his way down between my legs and started licking. Without warning, he abruptly stopped and took his shirt and pants off. His dick stood at attention, looking scrumptious.

I'd almost forgotten how strong my husband was until he picked me up and held me upside down then ate my pussy. I grabbed his dick, and we commenced our standing 69.

When he put me down, he lay back on the bed, and I mounted all nine inches of him. I started slowly, and he held my hips guiding me up and down. I picked up the pace, and it felt like I was going to cum at any moment. As I came, I heard the sound of my wetness, and I collapsed on top of him. He suddenly flipped me over and placed my legs on his shoulders. He got on his knees and rammed inside of me, working it this way until he couldn't take it anymore. His hot liquid poured inside of me, and I it hit me that I hadn't felt that good in a long time. Jock collapsed next to me and was snoring before his head hit the pillow good.

I woke up the next morning to see Jock staring at me. I instantly became nervous, scared that he felt something was different about his fit in me.

"You know, Nina, I love you. You are a wonderful mother and a helluva lover. I don't know how I haven't been damn near living in that pussy." He chuckled.

"Jock, I love you, our life, and your dick. You need to stop being so stingy with that shit," I teased.

"You right; I'm throwing out the calendar. That shit is played."

"It damn sure is," I agreed, satisfied with his decision.

Jock got up and headed toward the shower but turned around before going into the bathroom. "Oh, did I tell you that Chaz is moving to New York? He's going there to expand the business."

"Really? What about Shannon?" I was curious.

"I think he's going to ask her to marry him and take her and the baby."

"Oh, well, that's nice," I said dryly. I really was happy for Shannon; I was just a little disappointed the dick was moving so far away.

When we got to work, Chaz walked into my office and sat down.

"So, did Jock tell you about my move?" he asked.

"Yes, and I'm happy for you. I know New York is home for you; shit, its home for me, too. But my life is in Kentucky now."

"Yeah, it is. But you know, there are some things I'm going to miss about this place," he hinted with a smile.

"Well, Kentucky's always here if you ever decide you want to move back from the big city. You know, Jock could always use you here."

"Oh, only Jock now, huh?" Chaz joked.

"Well, I had a good time. It was something I needed, an itch that needed to be scratched," I explained.

"Listen, I hope the fun we had helped you and Jock in some way. I see that nicca singing to himself and humming all day, so I know you putting it on him right."

"Yes, things are good, Chaz. Thank you for helping me get my sexy back," I said in a low voice.

Chaz winked then headed towards the door. Before he walked out, he turned around and whispered, "It was always there, my nasty nymph Nina."

Chasing the Dragon

IT'S SAID THAT THE FIRST HIT PRODUCES a high but also a craving for the second one. And every hit after that is just chasing the feeling that the first hit brought. No, I'm not on any drug; well, I'm not snorting, smoking, or injecting anything. It seems that his sex has become my drug of choice; and no I'm not chasing the dragon per se, but I *am* chasing the dick.

His tongue traced the curve of my abdomen as he made his way along the bend of my hip. His mouth was like a river: His tongue was so moist, and it seemed to never to run dry. He moved to the outside of my leg and down to my toes; when he placed my big toe in his warm, wet mouth, I thought I would faint. He gently sucked each toe as he played between my legs like a well-trained pianist. My back arched as he played a quick tune, and I didn't think I could take it any longer. But just when I thought I'd reached my peak, he took my toes out of his mouth then threw my leg over his shoulder. He moved his hand up and down his big black dick, teasing me with each stroke; he knew I was starving for it. I scooted my pelvis toward him, and he thrust himself inside me. I gushed, both in excitement and juices.

"*Mimi! Mimi!*" I could hear him, but he sounded so distant.

I could feel pressure on my shoulder, like he was pinning me down while he plunged in and out. But then I heard my name being called more loudly. "*Mimi!*"

I shook uncontrollably as I melted all over his big dick.

"What's wrong with you?" I heard the deep voice ask. I felt the grip on my arm become tighter. I opened my eyes and tried to focus; I saw Rob sitting in bed next to me, staring in my face.

"Huh?" That was the only word I could muster up. I suddenly felt embarrassed, hoping I hadn't been performing too much.

"You were moaning and mumbling some incoherent shit. Are you okay? You sounded like you were being chased or something." Rob seemed concerned.

"Oh, it was just a dream, I guess. I don't even remember what I was dreaming about," I lied.

"Well, you better stop eating before bed."

"Yeah, you're right. Let me go get a glass of water; the heat's high in here, and it's drying my mouth out." When I stood up and started walking, I felt all the moisture pooled between my legs.

What the hell? I thought. I wondered if I would ever stop having these wet dreams about him… Probably not any time soon; he had been consuming a lot of my thoughts lately. I smiled when I reflected on how we became acquainted.

We met by chance, but our meeting seemed predetermined. I had my head down, walking and texting on a busy midtown street in Manhattan, when I collided right into him/ my cell phone slipped out of my hand, and in my attempt to catch it, my most treasured brown leather Dooney and Bourke® bag hit the ground, and I almost met both of them there. But I suddenly felt a strong clasp on my elbow that steadied me.

"Let me," he offered with an accent that let me know he wasn't American; he sounded like he was English. He bent down to pick up my things, and I was perspiring from sheer embarrassment.

"I hope you weren't in the middle of a business text," he said as he handed me my phone, which was in the process of rebooting.

I looked up into his eyes. I hoped he wouldn't notice that I was staring at him, no longer concerned with my phone or my most cherished bag.

"Ummm... oh, it wasn't an important text. I was actually reading a work-related email. I'm so sorry for bumping into you like that. Thanks."

I pulled my bag onto my shoulder and decided to walk away before I made an even bigger fool of myself. Before I did, I took a minute to take him in. I couldn't help but notice that he was as fine as they come: tall, dark, well-dressed and, judging from the few words we exchanged, well-spoken.

"No problem," he said then began walking away. He must've only taken a few steps because after I turned to keep walking, I heard, "Excuse me".

I turned to face him, the cold New York wind whipping my hair around my face.

"Yes?"

"Are you in a rush? Can I treat you to a hot latte?" he asked with a coy smile.

I paused before answering. "Sure, I have time."

I noticed his wedding band, and I was wearing mine, so there were no expectations with this little coffee "date."

We ended up at a quaint coffee shop across the street from where we were standing. As I sat at the table across from this oh-so-hot-chocolate of a man, I couldn't help but wonder why I'd even bothered to accept his invitation.

So what can I call you?" he inquired.

I don't know why, but I pulled out my business card. *"I'm Mia. Mia Michaels, and you are?"* I asked with a smile.

"Corey. Corey Alexander. I'm VP of Marketing at the Astra Euro Bank right up the street," he told me, taking his business card from the shiny silver case.

"Nice, Mr. Alexander. Thanks for not making me feel stupid for dropping everything at your feet this morning." I blushed and felt the heat rising to my still cold face.

"I'm actually glad you were texting and bumped into me. It gave me a reason to speak to you. I've seen you a few mornings; I mean, it's hard not to notice a beautiful woman, if I might say so."

The waiter came and took our coffee orders, and I thought it was cute that we both liked our lattes the same: lots of foam, extra hot, and with a shot of vanilla. As we spoke I watched his eyes search my face, and I noticed his eyes linger on my lips; I was doing the same to him. I loved the way his cheeks concaved as his dimples had their way with each smile.

An hour later, I still didn't have work on my mind, and it was obvious that he was in no rush to get to the office either. But the hour did provide us with enough time to learn a few things about each other. I learned he'd been married for the past seven years to a woman named Sarah; they had a son, Brock, whose nickname is Rocko, along with two dogs; and they resided in Greenwich, Connecticut. I shared that I, too, was married, and had been for five years to my college sweetheart, Rob and that we shared a handsome two-year-old son, Raymond, and we lived in Brooklyn. I ended our little meeting, promising to meet with him for lunch later that week. As I walked up the street to my office, I wondered if lunch with this handsome stranger was the best idea.

When I got to work, I sat at my desk, listening to voicemails and staring at his business card. I couldn't help but be intrigued by him. His accent was sexy, his smile, inviting, and from what I could see through his dress shirt, his physique was more than desirable. I alternated between picking the card up then putting it down for a few minutes. I was so caught up in trying to figure out what to do that when my phone rang, I nearly jumped out of my seat. It was my secretary, telling me I had a call on line one from a Mr. Alexander.

I told her to put the call through but stared at the phone for a few seconds before picking it up.

"Hi, Corey." Damnit! Couldn't I think of a better way to answer the phone than that? I leaned back in my chair, wanting to kick myself.

"Hi, beautiful. I know we just left each other, but I can't fight this feeling of needing to see you again – and soon. Can we do lunch today or an early dinner?"

I was already in Outlook, scanning my calendar before he could finish his sentence, to see how I could make time for Corey in my day. It was crammed with meetings and deadlines, so I decided we could meet for an early dinner.

"Well, Corey, it looks like my day is overbooked." I laughed. "But, an early dinner sounds great. Let me just make sure Rob can pick up Ray, and we'll be set."

"Great, I'll email you at the address on your card to send you a few restaurant suggestions. You pick which one you'd like to go to, and I'll make reservations," he offered without hesitation. Hmm…I thought to myself, I like a man that just takes control.

We agreed to meet at the Blue Fountain in Midtown, and I spent the last twenty minutes of my time at the office freshening up my makeup and smoothing out the crease in my slim-fitting pencil skirt.

When I walked in to the restaurant, I gave my name to the maître'd. But before the he could say anything, I saw Corey walking towards me from the restaurant bar. I smiled, and blushed, because he looked so fucking good. I watched him walk towards, and it was like he was literally approaching me in slow motion. I felt no shame about the puddle I was sure I was creating around my feet.

His navy blue suit fit his square shoulders nicely, and his white shirt was such nice contrast to his suit and his skin tone. His bald head shined in comparison to the dim restaurant lights. He even walked like he had a big dick with slightly bowed legs, and his feet were quite large.

"Mia," was all he said before planting a peck that lingered perhaps a second too long on my flushed cheek. I could feel the slight wetness from his lips, the heat from his body, and smell the scent of his enticing masculine cologne.

"Corey, I hope I'm not late."

"No, darling, you're right on time. I was just having a cocktail at the bar, while they prepped our table. But I just got the nod that it's ready." He held his arm out in the direction of our table. Something about the way he said "darling" made me want to sit in his lap instead of the seat at the table. During dinner, we couldn't keep our eyes, feet, or hands from touching. The energy between us was so thick that the small talk we tried to make about business fell on deaf ears for both of us it seemed. We sipped glass after glass of wine until I could no longer contain my desire to see him out of that suit.

"So, we have to do this again soon Corey," I said as I placed my hand over his. Fuck it, the expensive Chardonnay had me feeling brave.

Corey picked up my hand, and gently kissed it. On the back side, at first; but then, right there in the restaurant, he slipped my index finger into his mouth and slowly began sucking it. His warm mouth and fluid tongue turned me on instantly. I must've had my eyes closed, because I didn't even notice that the waiter brought the bill to the table.

When Corey gently placed my hand on the table to sign the receipt, I knew right then that I had to have him. He pulled out my chair from the table then assisted me with putting on my coat. We walked in silence up the block to the St. Regis. There was no need for words. I sat in the luxurious lobby as Corey booked a room for the night. I knew there was no way I could stay out all night, but I wasn't really worried about that at the moment. After he secured the room key, I walked by his side and we stepped into the elevator in silence. The heat was rising from my body was something I'd never experienced.

We got off on the 14th floor and walked down the long hallway to room 1435. I followed behind him after he opened the door. Before it even closed, I was pulling his long wool coat from his body. He turned around, and we engaged in a fight of sorts. I was pulling and tugging his clothes off his body, and he was doing the same.

His tongue explored my mouth so deeply, and he took turns sucking and nibbling on my top and bottom lips.

Corey opened my blouse, while I tried unbuttoning his shirt. Apparently, I wasn't taking his shirt off quickly enough because he pulled at the sleeves and flung it to the ground, exposing his tank top. In the turmoil, my blouse lost a button or two, but at that moment, I didn't care. He got what he wanted when my breasts spilled out of my push-up bra. He licked his way down my neck then cupped my breasts, fiddling with my erect nipples. Corey sucked one, then the other. Next, he hungrily pushed both of my breasts together, trying to suckle them at the same time. His tongue flicked against my hardened nipples causing my clit to tingle with each flicker of his touch.

He lifted my skirt up around my waist then yanked my pantyhose and thong down with one swift move. My own hands were traveling all over his body. Corey took his free hand and played with my swollen clit, and just when I thought I couldn't take any more, he stuck his middle finger in my warm, soaking wet opening.

"Ooh…oh, Corey! Oh…" escaped from my lips in a mere whisper. I could feel his bulge and decided I needed it at that very moment.

So, I unzipped his pants, and pulled it out. My assumptions were right: It was long and thick. With his pants around his ankles, Corey hoisted me up against the wall, and my legs straddled his waist. He quickly grabbed a condom from his pocket and put it on in a shaky rush. When he pushed himself in me, I thought I would faint, because it took my breath away. He felt so fucking good. The angle of his dick, the bend, curved into my body so perfectly. He pumped aggressively, and I used all the strength I had to climb the walls with my back for leverage for what I wanted to put on him.

"Mia! Why do you feel so good?" he whispered in my ear as he pumped away. Between my moans, his grunts, and the swooshing of my liquids against his thrusts, I'm sure anyone walking past our room door would instantly be turned on. Especially since we hadn't even made it all the way inside the room yet. We were in the alcove by the door.

"Corey!! Oh!" I yelled as I came all over him.

"Fuck, Mia! Fuck!" Corey muttered aggressively. He pulled out, holding the end of the condom, which was filled with his energy. He must've felt how weak my legs were from my explosion, because he slowly and gently let me down. I stood on my own two feet for the first time in five minutes, and I felt like I was just learning to walk. I felt ashamed for a moment, as I slowly walked over to the lavish king-sized bed with my totties flopping everywhere. I was a little slightly weak, so I lay back, trying to collect myself and take in what I'd just done. I knew I must've been sight to see with my pantyhose still around my ankles, but I didn't care. I watched him walk to the bathroom with his dick in his hands. I heard the water running, so I closed my eyes and reminisced on how he felt inside of me. My eyes flew open in shock at the lukewarm water on my crotch. Corey was sitting on the bed next to me, washing my vaginal area with a cloth. I started to sit up and say something, but he brought his index finger to my lips to hush me then gently pressed me back down on the bed. He gently nudged my legs open wider, and he gently, yet efficiently wiped my entire area. I got comfortable, closing my eyes to enjoy the gentle cleanse.

I felt him remove my pantyhose from around my ankles, and without warning, he began the most sensuous exploration. Holding my lips apart with one hand, he used his tongue to explore between my legs. He tasted me, gently at first, as I held on to his smooth head. Next thing I knew, he vigorously sucked my clitoris, making me feel like I was floating in outer space. His warm tongue teased my clit in a fast motion. Using gentle then hard strokes, he used his tongue as he did his dick, digging deep into my hole.

I cried out in ecstasy. "Please don't stop!" Every whimper and moan seemed to excited him even more as he feasted hungrily, I looked into see his eyes, just above my mound as he went in, showing me no mercy. Suddenly, he flipped me over onto my stomach; and I lay there, unsure of what was next. I jumped when I felt my ass cheeks open and his tongue exploring my asshole.

"Corey! No! No!" My protest became weaker as he gently held me down and licked with reckoned abandonment. Rob had not ever done that, and it was something I wasn't even into. But oh my, I couldn't deny that Corey's tongue was the truth, and it was telling me some things. After I shook, shuddered, and came with his tongue in my ass, I felt Corey's weight as he mounted me from behind. He entered my pussy, nerves still on edge from my orgasm, with a gentle thrust. I absorbed him entirely, and we gasped together, taking in the delicious feeling we were experiencing. Corey sucked my neck and licked what he could of my back as he pounded away, and my ass vibrated with each push. He found my mouth and decided I should taste myself.

He plunged his tongue into my mouth, and I sucked all my juices off as our bodies became entangled in a rivalry of lust. As we kissed, he reached around to stroke my face, and I grabbed his fingers, sucking two of them, never letting his tongue leave my mouth. I was hungry for him, and I wanted as much of him in me as I could fit at one time. I bucked back, throwing my ass at him, and he moaned between kisses. His pace quickening as he muttered my name.

Suddenly, he pulled out then exploded his warm liquid all over my ass. He wiped me with the same cloth from as he panted.

I watched Corey drift off to sleep. I didn't know about him, but I knew I had better be getting home. My business meetings generally didn't last this long, and I didn't want to hear Rob's mouth about me making work too much of a priority.

As I searched the floor for my undergarments, I wondered if Corey did this often, if I was just one of the many women he seduced regularly. A tinge of shame reared its ugly head at me, yet a sense of fulfillment came over me as well. I felt wanted, and my body felt more pleased than it had in years. I found my pumps and coat by the door, and just as I put my hand on the knob to open it, I heard his voice.

"Mia, don't leave without giving me a goodnight kiss." His sexy English accent made me want to go another round. I walked over and bent down to give my lover a deep, wet kiss, one that I hoped he'd think about on his way back to Connecticut.

"Are you going home tonight?" I was curious.

"Yes, I'll linger around here for a little, and then make my way to Grand Central for a late train, or I'll just call car service and to get home. Speaking of which, let me call you a car. There is no way I'm letting you get on the train. You must be drained."

With that, he pulled out his phone and hit what looked like a number on speed dial. He gave his corporate account number and told them I was going to Brooklyn.

I was impressed, but more importantly, I was happy for the ride home, because I was drained and needed the ride home to recuperate, both physically and mentally.

"How was your day, babe?" Rob greeted as he pecked me dryly on the lips. Before I could answer, he sat back down in front of the computer to continue his chat on Facebook.

"It was okay. Very busy," I replied, although he was no longer listening or interested.

I headed to Ray's room; I knew he was asleep, but I loved watching my baby sleep. He looked so sweet.

I peeled off my clothes, sniffing each garment for a hint of Corey. I found him on the collar of my blouse and held the shirt up to my nose and inhaled his scent. It made my body tingle as I reminisced on his tongue searching what seemed like every crevice of my body.

I showered slowly because spending the time in the shower felt like therapy. As I stood there, it felt as if my skin was sensitive to every drop of hot water that flowed from the large shower head. I could still feel his touch, and the thought of him made me caress my arms and my breasts, just for a moment. I needed to relive his touch before my shower ended and reality set in.

The next day, I sat in my office, wondering why I hadn't bumped into him this morning. I didn't want to call him, because I didn't want to seem pressed. I took it for what it was: a fling. A one-time thing that I shouldn't have done, but I oh-so-needed-to-do-yet-never-do-again. I was pensive as I stood up from my desk then sat back down. I didn't even realize how long I'd been staring out of my window until my secretary briefly knocked on my door before entering. *Why the fuck does you knock if your ass is just going to walk in anyway?* I asked.

But I turned and smiled, "Yes Ashley, what can I do for you?"

"Hi, Mia! I'm sorry to barge in."

I noticed that she was carrying a large bouquet of red roses in an expensive-looking crystal vase. Like a teenaged girl, I squealed with joy. When I saw the look in her eyes, I realized my behavior was kind of strange.

"These flowers are gorgeous! Rob isn't in the doghouse is he?" Ashley's prying ass inquired.

Without a response to her silly question, I just took the vase out of her hand. When I turned around and saw her still standing there like she was waiting for me to read the card to her, I dismissed her with a, "Thanks Ashley; unless you need me, that'll be all."

Ashley knew that she was about to cause the slight rise in the vein on my forehead and that she had about two minutes before I got in her ass, so she quickly dismissed herself.

I smiled widely for about two seconds before realizing that I must've looked like a fool. I had to smell the roses since they were so fresh and beautiful. I sat back in my seat and slowly opened the card with butterflies in my stomach. It read: *"My sweet Mia, words can't express what your company meant to me. I'd love to see you again. Soon. Warm Regards, Corey."* He wanted to see me again soon! That's exactly what I wanted to hear, because he was a skilled lover. His dick was so good; it was hard for me to rationalize why I should give it up since Rob had become less than erotic as of late.

I called Corey to thank him for the flowers, and he sounded so sexy, his words flowing out of his mouth like the smooth, melted milk chocolate used for dipping fruit.

"Mia, I'm glad you called. I'm glad you made it in to work safely; I've been thinking of you."

It wasn't what he said, but the way he said it, that caused my panties to flood with my lust for him.

"Corey, I've been thinking of you, too. I'd like to see you again soon." I couldn't believe I somehow had the nerve to be that forward with him. But lust does something to you, I suppose.

"Can we do lunch today?" he asked.

I quickly scanned my calendar, to see if I needed to move any meetings around so I could have a nice, two-hour window open for Corey.

"Sure; 12 okay?" I asked.

"Sounds fine. I'll have my secretary make reservations for us, and I'll email you the location."

"See you soon." I hung up the phone and walked over to the window again. My heart raced at the thought of sitting across from him again. I really was not all that interested in any meal; I just needed to feel him again. To soothe myself, I placed my hand on my chest, because it felt like I was having a panic attack. How could I not have him, but how could I?

When I walked into the dimly lit, swanky midtown restaurant full of patrons, I observed men in business suits conducting million dollar meetings over Cognac and filet mignon, women meeting with co-workers, and long lost friends catching up on their boring lives. I got seated and waited for my new friend to arrive. As soon as I saw him walking towards the table, I took a deep breath. He looked great, dressed in a dark gray wool overcoat and a navy double-breasted suit. I hoped my eyes weren't giving away my lusty desires. "Corey," was the only word I could form as he pecked me on the cheek and took a seat directly across from me.

We just sat and looked at each other for a few moments without saying a word. He finally reached across the table and touched my hand like an old lover; our eyes met, silently reminiscing about the previous night's escapade. There was, however, nothing to be said. The waiter arriving broke our lusty trance, bringing us back to the reality that we were sitting in a restaurant in the middle of Manhattan, mid-day, in the middle of the week. We could run into any business associate, friend, or family member, and the looks on our faces would say it all: that yes, we'd been intimate, and yes, that shit was good.

After placing my order for a grilled shrimp salad, I decided to excuse myself and retreat to the lady's room. I walked inside, nearly panting; he caused me to feel this intense rush. I ran my hands under the cool water for a few seconds and steadied myself with my hands on the sink. I heard the bathroom door open, and I damned myself for not locking the door... until I felt his body hovering over mine. I felt the heat from his breath on my neck, and when I looked up and into the mirror, I saw all his beauty.

Corey turned me around so I was facing him, then he placed an aggressively passionate kiss on my lips, parting my lips with his luscious tongue. We played tongue games, and his hands traveled along my hips, sliding my skirt up around my waist. I carefully turned around in the narrow bathroom, which was made for one person's use at a time and held on to the sink. He slipped my pantyhose down and moved my thong over to the side. I closed my eyes then braced myself for the feeling After I heard the zipper to his pants come down, Corey pushed himself in me so deeply, I swear I could feel my cervix shift. I tried stifling my moans of pleasure as he took turns steadying his ride using my hips and gripping my breasts through my shirt.

At first I didn't want to look in the mirror, because I thought I would feel some kind of shame, shame that I was letting this stranger – yes stranger-- enter my world. Letting him inside the place that only my husband had been since I met him 10 years before. Yet, as I reluctantly looked up at our reflection, I didn't feel shame. On the contrary, I felt sexy and wanted. I licked my lips as I watched Corey pump fast and hard. Beads of sweat formed across his forehead, so I knew he couldn't hold out much longer.

I couldn't hold out much longer either. I could feel it building up, while Corey fucked me wildly.

"Mia, Mia... oh shit," Corey whispered in my ear as his tongue traced my ear.

The walls of my pussy contracted and released forcefully as my body shivered from the explosive orgasm that overcame me. The warm liquid on my ass brought me back to reality. I watched Corey's tightly shut eyes and his tight mouth muting his own moans. Once he opened his eyes and came back to earth, he wiped his explosion off of my ass with the paper towels offered by the swanky restaurant. I watched him put his dick back in his pants and zip them, but when he went to pull up my pantyhose, I refused.

"I got it," I told him. The shame I was looking for earlier was now creeping in. I couldn't help but question myself: *I'm in a public restroom, getting the shit fucked out of me by a stranger I met a few days ago. A married stranger at that. What the hell has gotten into me?"* My thoughts were all over the place as I waited for him to make his way out of the ladies' room.

Between my time in the ladies' room and my walk back to our table, my appetite was gone, and I decided I needed to return to work – immediately.

"Look, sweetheart, our lunch is here waiting for us." Corey attempted to make a joke.

"Uh, you know what? I'm just going to get my coat and leave. I really need to get back to the office. I'm sorry I can't eat; I have to leave," I kind of rambled without looking him in the eyes or waiting for a response.

Over the next few days, I avoided his calls, but the weekend brought its own set of complications. I watched Rob, really watched him, for the first time in a while. He was a great dad, and Ray was his pride and joy. I could also see that Rob loved me: He cooked for me and took care of our home, but I wasn't sure if Rob saw *me*. It's like even when he looked at me, he wasn't really looking at me. And our conversation had become quite generic: our son, our bills, responsibilities, etc. Not much about either one of us or our needs. I wondered if anyone was enjoying Rob like I'd enjoyed Corey.

I sat on the couch next to Rob and tried to get into the movie he was watching, but my mind kept racing back to Corey. His touch was something out of this world, and he made my body feel something it hadn't felt in a long time. I just felt so sexy with Corey; I wondered if I could get that feeling back with Rob. There was at least some point in time that I couldn't get enough of him. *Couldn't we have that again?* I thought.

After the movie, I put Ray to bed and decided I would try to spark something with Rob. I mean, we still have sex, but it's so deliberate, almost like we're doing each other a favor t. So I showered then put on a pair of boy shorts and a sexy came. Rob had never really been one for the garter belts and other slower. He liked me to be relatively simple sexy, I guess.

I oiled up, and since I knew he wouldn't be coming to bed any time soon, I decided to bring the party to him. I threw on a pair of black pumps, switched my way out to him, and sat on his lap.

"To what do I owe this?" Rob asked dryly with his eyes glued to the TV.

"Well, I figured I'd get a little cute for my baby tonight," I explained then started placing kisses on his neck.

Although Rob continued watching TV, I was determined to keep going, even though the humiliation of him being more interested in the television than me. I decided to try and get his attention another way, dropping to my knees in front of him. And it worked.

He watched me intensely as I pulled out his semi-hard dick and stroked it to its full potential. Then, I went in, devouring it like my favorite ice cream. With his dick in my mouth, I played with his tip with my tongue. I looked up at him, and his eyes were still on me, no longer paying attention to the television. I played with his balls and sucked his dick like I was a Hoover vacuum cleaner.

It didn't take long for Rob to start fucking my mouth, without the thought that it was a mouth and throat and not my pussy. I gagged, but that only seemed to make him more aggressive. He pushed his hips forward in a methodical rhythm and held on to my head. I knew Rob was on the verge of Cumming, and just as he did, I pulled him out of my throat, and he shot his load all over me came. I thought that when he caught his breath, he would be ready for another round or at least help get me off. Instead, Rob patted me on the ass as he got up to go shower. I was hoping that the shower would refresh him, and he'd be ready to get it going.

"Did you like that baby?" I asked, lying on the bed, letting him get a nice view my ass.

"That shit was good, Mia. So good that I'm about to sleep like a motherfucking baby," Rob complimented as he made his way to his side of the bed. I watched, my eyes wide when he patted me on the ass, like he was petting a dog on the head, got under the sheets then quickly went off to sleep, snoring and all. I sat up in bed, wide awake; it was only 10:30. I needed a fix, but I knew I wasn't going to get it that night. I grabbed my cell then went into the hall and texted Corey:

When can I see you?

I held my breath and waited for his response. I wondered if he would, considering the way I ended our last meeting.

You're in Brooklyn? He texted back.

Yes.

Meet me at the Marriot, Brooklyn. Let's meet @ the hotel bar @ 2 p.m. tomorrow. Check-in time is @ 3.

I didn't know how I was going to get out and meet my lover, but I would find a way. I had to meet him. I would spend my entire night thinking of a way if I had to.

Ok, see you then. I finally responded.

I crept back to the bedroom with a smile of satisfaction on my face. Rob's slight was now okay. I was going to meet Corey tomorrow; I didn't know where I would to tell Rob I was going. But it didn't matter, because I knew I would cum.

The Marriott Brooklyn boasted all the charm of the Marriott Manhattan without the busy Times Square location. It also happened to be very close to my home in the heart of Brooklyn Heights. I loved my area. Being able to walk to the Promenade and see the water was a bonus to living in this part of downtown Brooklyn.

I took the escalator up to the hotel's bar with knots in my stomach. I ended up telling Rob that I was helping my girlfriend, Sasha, decorate her new apartment in Queens, and that we were doing dinner afterwards. He wasn't even interested enough to question it.

As I got closer to the bar, I wondered if I looked okay. It would be his first seeing me dressed casually. I had on a pair of dark denim jeggings with an oversized cream sweater and wide belt paired with brown over-the-knee boots. My hair was in a ponytail, and on my lips was a basic baby pink gloss.

I saw him seated as I approached the door to the bar. There were many tables with hotel guests munching on appetizers and having mid-day cocktails, so I did a quick scan to make sure I didn't recognize any of the faces. Corey smiled and stood up when he saw me.

"Mia, thank you for coming." He scooped me up in an embrace that caught me off-guard. I must've looked stunned because he quickly apologized. *"I'm sorry for the PDA, Mia; it's a natural reflex with you."*

I thought it was cute; he was so technical at times. I couldn't help but savor his delicious scent, and he looked so sexy in dark jeans and brown boots. His white button-down shirt and blazer made him look business-like, even on a Sunday afternoon.

"No, it's okay. I'm just kind of in my neighborhood, so I'm a little nervous," I explained as I took the seat next to him at the bar.

"What can I get you?" the bartender asked.

"Um, it's a little early in the day, but you know what? I'll take a Mojito, please," I managed to get out.

"Sir, can I bring you something else?"

"Yes, another gin and tonic," Corey replied without taking his eyes off of me.

"Mia, you're so beautiful. What am I going to do with you?" He placed his hand under my chin adoringly.

"I don't know, Corey. I don't even know what we're doing Why am I even here?" I asked rhetorically.

"Because you enjoy my company as much as I enjoy yours, Mia."

I smiled then sipped my Mojito. I waited for the bartender to step away before I began speaking.

"Let me ask you something?" I set my drink down. "Why me? You're married. Do you cheat on her often?" I blurted out.

"Okay, Mia. I'm going to be as honest as I can. I was attracted to you the moment I saw you. When we talked over coffee, I felt like the feeling was mutual.

"Yes, I'm married, and happily for the most part, if there is such a thing. I wouldn't leave Sarah for all the tea in China. We have a nice home and a great kid whose world I wouldn't want to turn upside down. Sarah's family is here, while mine is still mostly based in England, so she has a great support system, and they keep her busy.

"I will not lie though: I do find you quite charming and sexy. If I wasn't married, you'd be someone I'd consider having a relationship with. Have I had an affair before? Yes. A few years back, an old girlfriend from college and I hooked up a few times. But I don't have affairs regularly.

"I think we can appreciate each other's home life, and we can respect each other in a way that won't cause either one of us grief on the home front. Frankly Mia, we are going to enjoy each other, just as we have been."

I watched his lips move, listening. Before he could finish his statement, I had finished my Mojito and was motioning for the bartender to bring me another.

"Thanks for your honesty," I finally said. My one drink gave me just the buzz I needed to get over any nervousness I was experiencing.

"Corey, you must know I've never cheated on Rob before, so my feelings are all over the place. On the one hand, I feel bad for doing this, but on the other, I can't deny the way you make me feel," I told him, placing my hand on his thigh. This second mojito had me feeling ready.

"Would you like something to eat? Let me order you something." Corey was such a gentleman.

"Sure, an appetizer maybe." But it wasn't food I was hungry for.

We sat at the bar for the next hour drinking drink after drink, while nibbling on potato skins and each other's ear lobes. We were like two young lovers who couldn't keep their hands off of each another. Corey looked at his watch then smile.

"It's check in time baby," he whispered in my ear. The brush of his lips against my ear and the warmth from his breath made me tingle all over.

"You can wait here while I get the room key." I just nodded; he knew best.

I sat at the bar, anticipating the feel of Corey's flesh against mine. Within minutes, he was at my side, his hand on the small of my back. He must've known that I'd had more than reached my limit of drinks and that I would need assistance getting down from my stool. As I stepped down, all the mojitos I'd drank waved hello. I felt beyond tipsy, and I was drunk and ready to fuck.

I walked into the elevator like a champ, ready for the prize fight. I was determined to fuck Corey like it was my last opportunity to score a piece of his award-winning dick. At the end of the day, with our situation being what it is, I really didn't know how long we would be able to continue our little dalliances. When we got off on the fourth floor, I could feel the liquid courage taking over, I didn't have the best control of my legs. I was stumbling like it was 3 A.M. Instead of 3 P.M. The alcohol may have fucked up my equilibrium, but I knew exactly what I wanted

We entered the room like we had no time to waste, because we didn't. We both knew that, time was of the essence. I started pulling my sweater off as soon as we were on the other side of the door. Corey began kissing me as he walked me backwards to the bed then gently lay me down. He made a liquid trail from my lips to my breasts, swallowing my hardened nipples one at a time. He then licked his way down my stomach, stopping for a second to dart his tongue in and out of my navel. I thought he was going to pull my pants down with his teeth, and he certainly attempted to. I lifted my ass slightly to make his attempt easier; yes, I was eager. I opened my legs wide, wider that I'd ever had ever had them, and Corey opened my lips with his tongue. He sucked my clit gently at first then applied pressure. The pressure I'd been waiting for. The pace was so right; his tongue took long strokes up my entire line, even paying attention to the opening of my pussy. He sucked my juices like he was dehydrated and needed them to quench his thirst. My legs rested on his shoulders, and then he spread them as wide apart as my body would allow; he wasn't going be denied any drop of what I had to offer. At one point during his feast, you would've thought I was a trained gymnast with my legs forming a widely-opened scissor.

When Corey finally got enough, he simply lay back on the bed with his dick in his hands. There was nothing to say. I crawled up between his legs, and when I got to his dick, I opened my mouth as wide as I could before I attempting to swallow him whole. I placed my wet mouth on him then slid his dick in and out of my mouth; I used my hand to capture any part my mouth couldn't reach.

"You like having my cock in your mouth, don't you, Mia?" he asked between groans.

"*Mm hmm.*" I just nodded, because I wasn't taking it out of my mouth to answer. I fiddled with his balls and I felt them drawing closer to his body. I sucked like I was trying to get a thick milkshake through a small straw. I felt Corey's body tense up as he strained against the energy about to leave his body.

"*Oh, Mia! Oh!*" was all I heard before his cream erupted like a volcano. I watched the hot lava spill out of his body, and I assisted with a continuous stroke of my hand.

As I made my way to the bathroom to shower, I stumbled, slightly clumsy from the alcohol and the post climatic weakness of my legs. I held on to the bathroom sink to steady myself, then I rinsed my hands of his liquid. When I looked at myself in the mirror, what I was doing hit me: I was drunk, in a hotel with a man other than my husband, on a Sunday afternoon. The realization made me want to cry. In fact, tears welled up in my eyes, so I splashed my face with cold water, trying to rinse them away and hoping to sober up, all in one splash.

I stepped in the shower and braced myself for the hot water. Once inside, I washed myself off, feeling confused and regretful about my actions. As I was battling with myself emotionally about whether or not I should leave as soon as I got out, I felt a slight draft and then the warm skin of Corey's chest on my back.

He took my wash cloth and began washing my back, and I felt his dick growing against my ass. Corey's breath was on my neck as he reached his hands under my arms and massaged my breasts. Both my nipples and clit tingle from his touch. When he flicked his tongue on my neck, all of the guilt I'd been feeling vanished. I turned around to face Corey, and he tilted my chin so I would look into his eyes. How did he know I was trying to avoid his gaze?

"You okay babe?" he asked.

"I'm so fucked up right now, Corey," I admitted.

His response was to simply turn the shower off then usher me out carefully so I didn't slip. He grabbed the two waiting towels and wrapped one around me as if I were a child and wrapped one around his waist. He took me by the hand and led me to the bed.

"Sit down Mia," he commanded softly.

I plopped down on the bed and lay back.

"What's wrong baby? Why the sullen face?" Corey seemed concerned.

"I guess my alcohol is wearing off, and my conscience is kicking in," I said.

"Listen Mia, I don't want you to do anything you don't want to do."

"It's not that I don't want to do this. I do. I'm just a little sad that I actually got *here* in my marriage. What the hell happened?" I asked more to myself than him.

"Imagine this, Mia: You're with the same person for a long time. You're responsible for the same things, caring for your household and your child. There comes to a point when the spark you had becomes secondary to everything you have now. It's not a lack of love; it's a lack of spontaneity, the element of surprise, of desire, that dissipates.

"You know every move your husband's going to make. Every pump, how he's going to touch you, how long he spends kissing you before he moves on to the next part of your delicious body. We're only human. Could we make the choice to not go astray, and live completely mundane lives with the people we're promised to? Of course. But at the end of the day, as hard as we work, we deserve some sort of extracurricular stress relief," he finished, looking at me seriously

"So, I'm just an extracurricular stress reliever?" I scoffed.

"No, baby. You're not getting what I'm saying. Mia, I could be with any number of women; I'm here with you because I want to be. As beautiful as you are, your personality overrides your beauty. I actually enjoy talking to you as much as I enjoy tasting you." Corey leaned in and parted my lips with his tongue.

I opened my mouth to allow his tongue entry, and he climbed on top of me. We kissed slowly, as new lovers who weren't in a rush to go anywhere would. He opened my towel, and I could feel his heart beating against mine. His mouth left my lips and traveled to my neck. I don't know that I've ever felt lips as soft as his. He licked my neck so erotically, I started grinding into him. Corey then flipped me over on my stomach and kissed his way down the back of my neck. When he reached my ass, his tongue slid between my cheeks. I opened my legs wider, and he made a liquid trail from my ass to my wet opening.

"You taste so good, Mia. I could get fat with all this rich cream," Corey moaned.

"I want to feel you now, Corey. I need to feel all of you inside of me," I demanded. It felt like if I waited any longer, I would erupt. I scooted my ass up so that I was on all fours. Corey pushed me back down on the bed, and I heard the condom wrapper being opened. Before I could turn around, I felt the weight of his body on mine. He parted my legs with his knees and entered me from behind.

"Oh! Yes!" I gasped.

He pumped so deeply, and at first, we were so close that it felt like he was climbing inside of me. We grinded slowly in this position before it became animalistic. Corey motioned for me to scoot my ass up, so I was on all fours again.

"Cock it up, Mia." Corey demanded aggressively, and I followed orders. "Yes, that's it," he moaned as he banged away.

I pumped back feverishly, sweat beads forming on my forehead. His grunts let me know he was fighting the buildup and was about to erupt. I didn't fight mine; my body quivered, then I groaned in release. It was like Corey had been waiting on me because he immediately exploded into my now limp body. I was weak with exhaustion but instantly relieved of any stress I'd been feeling. I had a euphoric high I didn't want to come down from.

I watched the people 25 floors below, rushing to their destinations. For some reason, I wondered how many of them were engaging in extramarital or affairs outside of their relationships. I'd never given it much thought; I guess because it was something I never thought I'd be engaging in.

I tried not to think about Corey so much and remember that it is what it is: just two people helping each other fill a void present in their "real" lives. Whatever that meant, since Corey had made it pretty much clear that that's what it is. But I really did respect him for not bullshitting me in any way.

Having Corey in my world made my days easier, it seemed. I could deal with my home life with a smile, or at least I could fake a smile more easily. The fact of the matter is, lately, I'd been spending more time daydreaming than living in reality, the reality being I was fucking my way out of my marriage both emotionally and physically.

My thoughts were interrupted when my secretary let me know I had a call on line two from a Mrs. Charles.

"Mrs. Charles? In reference to?" I asked, confused.

"She said it's personal." My secretary said matter-of-factly.

"Well then, put her through. Thanks."

"This is Mia. How may I help you?" I asked after I picked up the phone.

"Hello, Mia. This is Sarah Charles Alexander."

My stomach dropped, and my mouth went dry instantly. I swallowed hard before I spoke. I immediately recognized who she was from her accent and last name.

"How may I help you?" My voice was shaky.

"Well, Mia, you can help me by not fucking my husband. That's what you're doing right?" Sarah asked, her voice laced with contempt.

"Excuse me, uh Sarah. I don't think this is the time nor place for this conversation. Frankly, I think you're having the conversation with the wrong person, anyhow," I responded, feeling annoyed. *How dare she call me?*

"Well, I don't think any time would be good for this conversation. But I just have one thing to say, and then I'll let you go about your day. Just remember you're dealing with a married man! He's *my husband, My world!* You are *nothing* but sex to him, and that's all you'll *ever* be! Remember that before you go getting any crazy ideas, your harlot!"

I wasn't about to sit there and let her curse me out, so I just hung up without saying a word. Besides, I didn't want her husband for anything more than a good time anyway, right?

I threw on my wool coat and headed towards the door, since I'd already sat at work way past quitting time anyway. Just when I stepped out, my phone buzzed, and when I looked down, I saw it was a text from Corey.

Meet me at the W in 15 mins. I have a table reserved for us. See you soon.

I looked at the message, wondering how he knew I was still in the city. I smiled to myself as I thought about how cocky he was to just assume that I'd just be available to see him at a moment's notice. Who the hell does he think he is? With that, I texted Rob:

Working late on a project. Don't wait up.

Fifteen minutes later, I was sitting across from Corey, watching his lips move, yet imagining them on my ear, my neck, his tongue in my navel.

I suddenly blurted out, "Your wife called me today."

Corey smiled slyly without flinching. "She did, did she? Well, don't worry; it won't happen again. Sarah loves to try to intimidate those she sees as a threat. I hope you weren't cruel in your response?" He said more as a question with his eyebrow raised. He sipped his Cognac.

"Of course not. I really didn't say anything; I actually just hung up. I didn't know what to say, because I've never been approached like that. I'm not exactly used to engaging in affairs with married men. Or any men for that matter." I watched him closely.

"Well, love, there's a first time for everything, and that time is now for you – and for us." Corey was so smooth.

"Are you full?" He asked. Without waiting for an answer, he grabbed my hand then stood up. I guess he was ready for the main course of the night.

When we walked into the suite and started to step out of my shoes, Corey sighed.

"Oh no, babe. You're keeping those on." He unzipped my dress in the back while kissing my neck. As he pulled the zipper down, he placed kisses on the exposed skin until he reached my tailbone. I was snapped out of my high by the ringing of my cellphone. I saw my home number flash across the screen and thought I'd better answer it, just in case there was an emergency.

"Hello Rob... Yes, I'll be home soon... Tell him I love him and that mommy will be home soon... I have to go; I have people in front of me." I pressed the end button on the phone as I felt my dress and panties being pulled down from my hips. Once they hit my ankles, I stepped out of them.

My back was still to Corey as he unhooked my bra; I let that drop, too, and his large hands cupped my breasts. He was breathing hot air into my ear while groaning. He played with my nipples, twisting them in between his fingers gently. I could feel his dick standing hard between my ass cheeks. Corey began licking my neck, and it felt so good that the warmth and wetness of his mouth mirrored the effect he was having between my thighs. He grabbed my chin forcefully, and my neck was sideways as he shoved his tongue into my mouth then licked and nibbled on my lips. With an aggressive push forward, my hands met the dresser, and I heard Corey undoing his belt. I didn't hear him take it off, but I felt the sting of the leather against my ass. It stunned me for a second but then I felt my nipples get even harder and my clit swell more. As Corey struck me with lashes on my ass I moaned with delight. It was hard enough to sting, but the prickle was just enough to turn me on in a way that I'd never been turned on before. I then heard the condom wrapper open, and within seconds, he was inside of me. I pushed back forcefully, wanting to feel him as deeply as I could. I steadied myself on my heels because he was pounding me like he had something to get off his chest. My breasts jiggled with every stroke, and my ass clapped against his groin, getting louder with each thrust.

"Oh goodness, Corey! I'm about to let go; you feel so fucking good! You give me such a high!" I complimented through gritted teeth.

"Take this dick, Mia! Take it!" Corey replied. His finger was pressed on my asshole, then he started moving it in and out. It felt so intense. Next, he reached around to play with my clit. I instinctively spread my legs further to give him easier access. Within seconds, my pussy tightened and released all over him.

"You've been working late an awful lot lately," Rob said without turning away from the monitor. When I pecked him on the side of the head, I could feel his not-so-positive energy. He was clearly not interested in my peck or my excuses. It had been three months, and I'd found a reason every week to get home late or go out more. I was not only neglecting my husband, but deep down, I knew I was taking the energy I should've had for my son and giving it to Corey.

Winter had set in, and as the New Year was approached, I couldn't help but wonder if I was ready to bring in another calendar year, chasing behind someone else's man while not investing in my own. Something had to give – and soon.

"By the way, if you think you can spare some time for me, we were invited to a New Year's party by Lee. It's going to be in the city, and I'm sure since you like to spend so much time there, you won't mind going," Rob quipped sarcastically.

"Sure, sounds good. I'll start thinking of something to wear. We'll have to get a babysitter now, you know."

"Done. I've squared that away already. I figured even if you decided not to go with me, you'd be out running around with work or something else on New Year's eve," he replied, staring in the eyes.

"Nope, honey; I'm all yours," I promised without returning his eye contact. Marched past him and into my son's room. I watched Ray sleep, leaning against his closed door for support. My heart wanted everything in this house, but my body wanted something else. I wiped away tears before kissing my son's forehead then sat on his bed, wondering how I'd gotten to this point.

I picked up my cellphone then put it back down. I'd taken a long hot shower, trying to wash off any last remnants of Corey. This habit, similar to that of a drug habit, had to stop; and I knew the only way I would be able to was to quit cold turkey. A 12-step program would only lead me back into his arms and eventually, his bed.

I watched Rob sleep thinking about where I went wrong with him. Had I focused on work too much? Why had it been so easy to fall out of love with him? I thought of Sara and how she must hurt, picturing the man she loved enjoying the pleasures of another woman. I picked up my phone again and texted Corey:

"I can't do this anymore. Please don't ever contact me again. I can't lose what's important to me. Thank you for everything. But I'm no longer chasing that high."

I put my phone on my nightstand hoping that I could stick to the message that I just sent him. I laid down and tried to muffle the sound of my cry as the realization of what I had done set in. Was I crying for what I did to my marriage or because I knew that I had just let go of the relationship that left me filled with so much ecstasy.

Summer's Heat, Inc.

"SOMETIMES, YOU JUST NEED A LIL SOMETHING else. A little variety. Shit, I like pizza, but I don't care how many toppings I try, I want a hamburger sometimes," Leon said, pontificating as usual.

"Yeah, I feel you, Lee. I'm just not trying to mess up what I got at home, man. If she ever found out I was fucking around, that would be it. I love my wife, and the life we've built. Shit, pussy is good, and new pussy is even better, but am I willing to lose everything for it? Fuck nah," I explained then sipped my Heineken.

"This is what I'm trying to tell you, man; listen to me. You see, y'all got the game fucked up. Dudes out here trying to have bitches on the side, bitches that want to be wifed. These the same bitches end up calling your wife, showing up at your crib 'n shit, blowing up yo' motherfuckin' phone when you chillin' with yo' fam. Nah, see that's where niggas go wrong. You can get your pussy – shit I believe it's every man's right! You work hard you should be fucked the way you want to be fucked." Leon paused and took a swig of his Henny; he loved to lecture.

"But, you got to do your shit right. There's the right way, man, and there's the sloppy way. You remember my man, Ty? He locked up on some bullshit, but he just put me on to his new business. He got his bitch runnin' that shit like a well-oiled machine, and let me tell you somethin', that dude is one smart motherfucker."

"Ok?" I was ready for his ass to get off the soap box and come with it. Leon pulled out his wallet and reached for a business card.

"You see this here?" he asked. "This is the drama-free way to have your cake and eat that shit, too. Fuck being on a diet! I, myself, have sampled every bitch on the menu, and let me tell you, this is top of the line pussy, and you get to choose your flavor. It ain't cheap, but I know you gettin' paper, so you good."

I picked up the card and examined it. It read "Summer's Heat" and was a simple, white business card. No women posing provocatively, just plain and non-descript with black scripted lettering.

"Summer's Heat? What's this? Some prostitution shit?" I needed to know. Shit, I wasn't about to stick my shit in some chick that stands on the corner in heels.

"Call it what you want. Men pay for pussy all the time," Leon pointed out. "What's the difference in getting straight to the point? Now you ain't gotta wine and dine a bitch to get no ass. You pay, they play, and they play well.

"There's only about five or so chicks: a blond Becky, you got a caramel sister, an Asian-Black mix, a dark skinned sister, and then there's the chick who's running the shit now, Summer. Now, they all bad bitches, and they can all suck a mean dick, but Summer is fine as hell, and her pussy good. Try 'em all, shit. It's like Baskin motherfuckin' Robbins: Pick your flavor." Leon was cracking up at his own joke.

I looked at the card again. "I'll give it some thought, Lee. It would be cool to feel some new pussy, but I don't know about all this, my dude."

I looked at the card again and thought about my marriage. I love my wife, but damn, things ain't been jumping off in the bedroom for a while. I took one last look at the card before sticking it in my wallet. *Hmmm, Summer's Hea*t, I thought out loud.

"Do yourself a favor and call, man. Think of it as a drama-free way to get that nut you need. Call, and ask for Summer," Leon tried convincing me as he tapped his Henny glass to my Heineken bottle, in a cheers motion.

I watched her. Studied her. My wife, as beautiful as the day I met her on our college campus. She was preparing for bed, rubbing oil all over her skin, rambling on about her nosy secretary or some random weird thing that happened on the train.

Then it happened, she pulled *my* t-shirt over her head, pulled on my flannel pajama bottoms, and threw on her Aunt Jemima scarf. And my dick went limp. This was it. This is what I was in for, for the rest of my life. Going to bed with Aunt Jemima by my side. She hardly ever even attempted to look sexy in the bedroom anymore. I'd ask, and she'd claim she was tired and always promised to throw some sexy back into our routine, but those promises had yet to be fulfilled. And I'm tired of feeling guilty for not getting a boner when she thinks I should have one.

Now don't get me wrong, my wife still has some of the best ass I've ever had; but shit, I'm tired of rolling over and fucking a corpse, an Aunt Jemima-looking corpse at that. So instead of getting in her guts like I used to, I'd just lay there and hold her before we drift off into our individual dream worlds. She seemed happy and satisfied with that cuddling shit.

I'm not trying to go nowhere; I've got my wife and my son, and that's all I really live for. But I need to dip and get some of this out. Like my man Leon said, it's my right as a man. It's every man's right as far as I'm concerned. I take care of home, and now, it's time to take care of me.

It had been about a week since I got the card from Leon. I had tried imagining my wife was some video dancer I lusted after from my favorite magazine, and I even attempted to have sex with her outside of our bedroom, but none of it made me feel like I was getting my needs met.

I sat in my cozy home office and dialed the numbers on the card, pressing them slowly as if my delay was somehow a way of convincing my dick that it didn't need no other pussy, all to no avail. The phone rang three times before a sultry yet sweet voice answered, "Hello?"

"Uh, yeah, um can I have Summer? I mean can I speak to someone named Summer?" I didn't know the right way to ask for someone to suck my dick.

Her giggle made her sound young. "This is Summer; how may I help you?"

"I was given your card by a friend. I'm interested in utilizing your services."

Meanwhile, I really was thinking, *I want some top-notch pussy.*

She paused for a second. "Hmmm, I take it this is the first time you've used a service such as mine. What do you have in mind? You want a woman of a certain persuasion? Group activities, someone to whip your ass before making you cum?" She didn't giggle this time; in fact, she sounded quite business-like.

I was stunned for a moment; I certainly didn't want anyone beating my ass, and I certainly had nothing against the Becky's, but I wasn't fantasizing about banging one of them out. I'd had my days with them back in high school. No, what I wanted was a fine sista, so I decided to tell her just that.

"Listen, I just want a fine sista who knows how to make a man's fantasy come true."

Without hesitation, and with a huff like I was taking up precious time, she asked, "Light, dark, caramel?"

I thought about it quickly then said, "Surprise me. As a matter of fact, Summer, you came highly recommended. I'd love to see you."

"My price is slightly higher than the other girls, if you have financial concerns."

This time I chuckled. "No, money is of no concern."

"Well, that's what I like to hear; you have the dime, I have the time. Let me open up my calendar and see what I can do for you, baby. Do you like to be called Zaddy?" she purred through the phone.

"You can call me Zaddy or whatever you want," I told her, my dick getting hard.

"Okay, Zaddy sounds good. But for my records, what's your name?"

"Rob. I like hearing you say Zaddy, but my name is Rob. Rob Michaels."

◖◗

I booked a room at the W Hotel near Union Square. I have to admit; I was actually nervous but not nervous enough to cancel my appointment. Besides, she had the nerve to charge a cancellation fee, and I wasn't paying to not to get any pussy.

I tried to imagine what Summer would look like, and I hoped I would get my money's worth. I was shaken from my thoughts, watching my wife get ready for work. She had the same routine every day. Every. Fucking. Day. I didn't have any homes or apartments scheduled to show today, so I was free until it was time to pick up my son, Ray, from daycare, and that was at six.

After my wife left the house, I showered and headed out to the city. I hated parking there, but I presumed today, it would be worth it. I checked into the hotel and paced around the room. After observing the view from the large window, I pulled back the bedspread to check the sheets. I still had an hour before Summer was scheduled to arrive, and since the anticipation had my dick hard, I decided to get one off before she got there.

I took my pants off and opened my cellphone. It was full of random porn pics my friends sent through our group chat. I got fixated on one caramel ass and went to work. I started with slow strokes of my dick as I imagined the faceless woman's fat ass sliding down on it, then I increased the pace as I thought she would. It didn't take long before I soiled the hotel carpet with my seed. Once I came down from my temporary high, I checked and rechecked my coat pocket for the condoms I'd bought at the local pharmacy. I hadn't used condoms in years, not since the night of my bachelor party. I hopped in the shower, and just as I was stepping out, I heard a knock at the door. It was her.

I opened the door, and my fantasy walked in. She had curly blond hair, creamy tan skin, luscious pouty lips, eyes that seemed like they saw through you, nice titties – not too big, not too small – and a nice, round ass. She was hot, hot like your hottest summer day.

"Hi, Rob," she greeted as she walked in, removing her coat with one sweep of her hand. I was still standing there, holding the door open, stunned by her beauty. She was like a mix of Beyoncé and Angelina Jolie.

"Baby, come here." Summer suggested in a sultry voice as she held out her hand to me.

I walked to her like a good boy.

"Lover, you seem tense. Let me help you with that."

With one flick of her wrist, she removed my towel and exposed my already throbbing dick.

I watched Summer drop to her knees. Then, she pulled a rubber from her thigh high, slipped it on with her mouth, and put my tip in the back of her throat. I just stood there, looking crazy. I couldn't say shit.

"Damn, you love this dick?" I asked as I ran my fingers through her curly hair.

"Mmm hmmm." The vibrations from her response felt amazing.

"Yeah... suck this dick. You want to swallow this dick?" I asked as if I really wanted an answer.

Without warning, Summer took my dick out of her mouth and started licking my balls. Then she put both in her mouth and sucked on them gently while using her hand to stroke my waiting dick. My eyes rolled in the back of my head due to the unbelievable feeling. I reached down and grabbed her titties, which were spilling out of her bustier. When I found her hard nipples, I circled them with my fingers, playing with them like a new Christmas toy. Summer's mouth felt hot and wet, even though the condom. She massaged my dick with her tongue, taking long deep strokes with her mouth wrapped around it. I looked around the room, trying not to look down into her eyes. Her eyes told me she enjoyed giving me this pleasure. I grabbed the back of her head and began fucking her beautiful face. Initially, she gagged slightly, but then she kind of smiled. Her smirk made me pump harder, determined to wipe the smile off her face. Summer was a professional, though; it seemed like her throat opened up to meet my thrusts, and her tongue circled the tip of my dick.

I came with such a force that my toes damn near broke from curling so hard, and my shoulders hunched when I tried to steady myself. It felt like I poured a pound of nut out of my sack. And it was a long awaited feeling.

When I opened my eyes, I saw that Summer had come off her knees and was sitting on the bed, smiling at me.

"Go take off the condom, shower up, then come relax with me," she almost ordered.

I was still trying to come to from that explosion, so I just nodded and went to the bathroom to get my shit together. After I flushed the condom, I stepped in the shower, feeling brand new. *Damn, Lee was right. I could get used to this shit,* I thought to myself.

I got out of the shower to find Summer laying across the bed with her back to me and her bare ass out. I didn't think my shit would be able to get hard again today until I saw Summer's ass sitting right there, inviting me in. I stood there, taking it in for a few moments, and I knew she could feel my presence.

"You like what you see?" She spoke without turning around.

"Hell yes, I do," I said, perhaps a little too eagerly.

Summer scooted backwards onto all fours, giving me a total view of her asshole and opening, the pink of her pussy so neat and tight-looking. I dropped my towel, determined to get every penny's worth of my money. My dick was rock hard again, and I began stroking it like I was watching a live porn. She turned over onto her back and started playing with herself. It was like she knew just what I wanted to see. Summer worked on herself as if she was in the room alone, but she didn't take her eyes off me. I sat on the bed next to her and jerked my dick; it was the livest porn I'd ever watched. I = inhaled her delicious scent and watched the area between her legs become shiny with her moisture. When Summer moaned, enjoying her own pleasure, I decided that I wouldn't waste my nut on the bedspread. I grabbed a condom from the dresser, never taking my eyes off of her. The anticipation of being inside her had the tip of my dick oozing with preliminary jazz. Since her legs were wide open, I lay over her, rubbing my tip on her clit.

"Fuck me, Rob. I need that big cock!" Summer demanded.

I placed her right breast in my mouth, playing with her nipple with the tip of my tongue before entering her. I felt her walls contract as I delved in deep. I stroked slowly, because I knew it wouldn't take long for me to buss.

The pressure built up quickly as I pumped in and out. Between her warmth and tightness and the sounds she was making, I knew I couldn't hold it in any longer, so I pulled out just before I exploded.

Summer must've sensed what I was feeling, because she motioned me to lay down on the bed. She licked from my ankles up to my lips, leaving a trail along my body. When she mounted me, I closed my eyes. Seeing her beautiful face and flawless body kept me on the verge of exploding. Moving slowly, Summer rode up and down in a wave of ecstasy. Then, she started winding her hips around on my rod and picked up speed, rotating her pelvis in a way that looked like she was ready to burst. I felt her fluids before I heard her voice she whimpered and slowed her speed. I was too far gone. I grabbed her waist and fucked her from underneath until I felt every drop leave my tip. She fell onto my chest, both of us trying to catch our breath.

I closed my eyes for what felt like a few minutes. When I opened them, I saw Summer about to exit the room.

"Rob, you were fantastic. I hope we can do this again soon; I have your credit card on file."

With that, she walked out of the door. I stared at the ceiling, realizing that I'd just paid for the best piece of punani I'd probably ever had. I lay there for a little while longer before I rinsed off and headed home feeling like a brand new man.

I couldn't wait to use Summer's services again. I knew she had other women who could service me, but I didn't mind the upcharge for Summer's heat. Life seemed to be just a little bit easier, plus I felt lighter on my feet. I was even more turned on than usual, and the thought of Summer had me giving Mia more dick than usual, too.

I met up with Leon and my boys to watch the Giants game at our usual spot. I wasn't going to bring up the fact that I'd used his advice, but he did.

"Man, did you take me up on that?" Leon looked over at me.

I tried to play it off, but I could see my boys looking at me, waiting for an answer. We had all been friends for years, so I knew it was all good.

"What advice you talking about, man? You always giving a nig advice, so clarify." I tried playing dumb.

"You know exactly what the fuck I'm talking about!" Leon laughed. "You get some new ass or what?"

"Oh that. I'm good, man. I'm *definitely* good," I offered without getting into details.

"My man!" Leon reached out to give me a pound.

I didn't have to say any more. We all held up our beers and nodded in acknowledgment that we all knew what was good. As I downed the last of mine, I made a mental note to schedule another session with Summer – and soon.

"Rob. Rob. Rob! Hellooo! Are you there?" Mia must've been trying to get my attention for a minute.

"Yeah, I'm here." I laughed it off. "What's up?"

"Oh. You seem distracted these days. Is everything okay?" Mia looked concerned.

"All's well, Mia. You tripping." I brushed her off. I couldn't help but think about the feel of Summer's lips around my dick.

Later that night while Mia was giving me her usual lackluster head, I closed my eyes and imagined it was Summer. Even though she always used a rubber while sucking, that shit was so good, I still got off fast. Mia jerked it and spit on it, trying to get me to cum fast; I'm guessing so she could feel like her job was done, and she could put that rag on her head and go to sleep. Tonight, I decided to help her along by me replacing her face with Summer's and quickly blasting off all over her mouth.

As I wiped the excess nut from my tip, I decided to schedule my next session.

The weather was just turning really cold as December came in playing no games. I wanted to grab a drink in the hotel lounge before going up to the room I'd booked for my rendezvous Summer, so I told her to meet me there. I should've known she had arrived when I saw all the businessmen's eyes widen as they looked the door. I turned to see the long-legged Summer with her blond, curly hair blown straight, saunter in with a full-length mink damn near dragging the floor. I stood up, watching her stroll over slowly, ensuring that everyone got a full view of her exquisite beauty. My dick grew hard against my pants as I gazed at her. When she arrived at the table, I pulled out her seat, and she pecked me on the cheek before removing her fur and sitting down.

"Rob, you look great, and I love your scent. Let me guess, Burberry?" Summer asked seductively.

"Yeah, that's exactly it. And you look beautiful as always. What can I get you?" I motioned for the waiter, who appeared quickly.

"Cabernet blanc would be nice."

It was quiet for a few minutes as we sat there. I really didn't know what we could talk to about, but I was curious about her in a strange way.

"So Summer, if I may ask, what's a gorgeous girl like you doing in a business like this? You could be on the cover of any magazine."

She smirked and sipped her wine before answering.

"Thanks for the compliment, Rob. That's nice of you to say, but I'd like to keep my business to myself. I mean, I could ask you why a fine man such as yourself would even be entertaining someone in this business. But I won't. So let's just enjoy each other's company and stick to the business at hand. Besides, I actually *like* fucking you, so it's just a bonus that it's actually my job." Summer giggled as if she hadn't just put me in my place.

"Okay, cool." I downed my Cognac and eyed Summer's smooth thigh peeking at me from under her short skirt. Her tall boots hit right above her knee, giving me just enough of her thigh to put my hand on. She smiled when I placed my hand there and slid it slowly up her skirt just a bit.

"You ready to go upstairs, I see," Summer whispered.

"I was ready when you walked in."

I paid my tab and ushered Summer to the elevator. I was behaving like a single man on a date with his new girl. I felt young, free, and with Summer on my arm, I felt like "the Man!"

When we entered the room, Summer excused herself to the bathroom. I took off my clothes in a hurry and lay on the bed with my arms behind my head. Several minutes later, she came out of the bathroom, wet from an apparent shower, and she didn't even bother to wrap herself in a towel. My dick sprang to attention at the sight of her body. She looked like fresh cream, soft and sweet. Her breast sat up perky, and her pinkish-brown nipples were already hard, like she'd been playing with them while she was in the shower. She stood still for a few seconds, watching me watch her. The sun coming through the hotel window made her glow even brighter.

"Rob. Tell me what you need. Do you like what you see?" Her voice was low and seductive. How could I *not* like what I saw? Couldn't she tell from the way my dick stood up like a pole sticking out of the ground that I liked what I saw?

"You can't tell?" I asked playfully, pointing towards my dick. She looked down then licked her lips like she saw something delicious.

Summer leaned back against the hotel dresser and opened her legs. "Come here, Rob."

I did as she asked, and when I stood in front of her she put her hands on my shoulders and gently pushed me down. I kneeled in front of her and opened her pretty pussy with my hand. I just needed to look at it for a moment before inserting my tongue deep inside her and tasting her sweet juice. Summer opened her legs wider as she moaned and wound her pussy against my face. When I sucked her fleshy bell, she yelped, and it sounded like music to my ears, so I kept going until she flooded my face with her splash. I came up for air, only to put one of her nipples in my mouth, while I played with the other. Then, I stuck my tongue in her mouth and kissed her like I used to kiss Mia in the early days of our relationship.

I grabbed a condom and turned her around so that she faced the dresser; she eagerly bent over. I went in slowly, feeling every ridge and crevice in her sweet spot. It was so wet, so gushy. I long stroked her, watching her ass ripple with each pound. I grabbed her hair from behind and yanked her head back. She seemed to take pleasure in that, because she began talking shit.

"That's all you got?! I thought you had some man in ya!" She snickered laugh.

That was all I needed to hear to go harder. I pounded her cakes while holding her waist with one hand and her silky hair with the other. It was like I was riding a horse, and I fucked her until my dick decided it couldn't go any longer. I held on tight until I felt emptied of all my stresses, leaving my hand print on her light skin. I wasn't paying to make love; I could do that at home.

Summer and I showered together, taking turns wiping each other down. We got in the bed, and I ordered some fresh fruit and juice from room service since we were both thirsty and needed the boost. Once we downed our refreshments, I was ready for round two. I intended to go home with my balls empty. Right when I began licking her ear, I heard a knock at the room door. I kept my momentum, licking her neck then traveling towards her ear.

"Let me get that," she suggested.

"I'm not expecting anyone. Let them knock," I whispered and kept licking.

Summer acted like she didn't hear me and walked toward the door completely nude. She opened the door wide without even asking who it was. In walked a beautiful, brown-skinned woman who also donned a black floor-length mink. When she got all the way inside, she opened her coat and placed her hand on her hip like she was awaiting my appraisal. I saw that she, too, was butt naked, her body a beautiful bronzed caramel tone but solid and thick. I smiled, and my dick showed its approval.

"Today's your day, Rob. A bonus for you; you think you can handle it?" Summer asked.

I didn't answer her; instead, I grabbed the bronze beauty and started sucking on one of her breasts. As my tongue circled her nipples, she threw her head back and dropped her coat. I grabbed a handful of her ass before leading them both to the bed. I lay on the bed, then the big brown ass straddled my face. Summer kneeled before me and began working her jaws. She put both my balls in her mouth and sucked on them gently as she stroked me with a hand. I delved my tongue deep into the big brown pussy sitting on my face. Her moans told me she enjoyed what I was giving her. Summer stopped sucking my balls for a brief moment and positioned herself with her ass in the air before she continued sucking my dick. Judging from Summer's moans, she was enjoying the caramel cutie's tongue that explored her walls. All three of us enjoyed this until the brown bottom came in my mouth.

I wanted to be inside of her, so I flipped her onto her back. Summer opened a rubber, placing it on me with her mouth, deep throating it until the condom reached the base. I placed the thick brown legs on my shoulders then plunged all eight of my inches deep inside her. He felt like a warm, creamy sponge, and with every stroke, I felt her walls tightening around my shaft. Summer played with her friend's titties, squeezing her nipples while playing with herself. We climaxed simultaneously with pretty brown cumming first, I letting myself go in her. Then Summer cumming as she watched me shudder.

"Rob, wake up!" I was being shook slightly.

"Oh, what time is it?" I wiped my eyes, trying to see the clock in our living room.

"It's just after seven. You must've had a hard day, a lot of clients," Mia stated, not really asking. I yawned, still trying to wake up.

"Yes, it was a busy, hard day, honey. I think I may have a few things lined up to sell soon, some nice property, too."

I rested my head on the back of my couch and smiled to myself, thinking about my day. I pulled out the card Leon had given me just a few months ago. I shook my head, reminiscing. "Summer's Heat Inc. What an investment in my marriage," I muttered.

"What was that, honey?" Mia called out from the bathroom.

"Oh nothing, honey. I just was talking to myself, saying I'm glad I'm so vested in our marriage." I smirked.

Breakfast with Peter

"Slow down, Sara. What is that, your third slice of pizza?" He asked as he always did. He called it, taking care of me, yet it was more like my punishment for holding on to the extra 20 pounds after the birth of our son. I could see it in his eyes, or should I say the lack of the look in his eyes: He'd become less than enchanted with me over the last couple of years.

"I bought you that gym membership three months ago. You still haven't seemed to be able to get there. Leave Rocko with your mum instead of sitting home, watching these talk shows while eating bagels, get your bum to the gym. I don't care about the extra weight you're carrying around, but it's so unhealthy." He told me the same thing at least once a week.

I tossed around the fact that he barely touches me anymore, and that he's immersed himself in "work" now more than ever. I decided that perhaps if I lost the 20 pounds or so, he would find himself in love with me again.

Eventually, I called my mum and asked her to free up three mornings per week for me so I could drop off Rocko and head to the gym. My mum didn't do anything but shop with her extra time. If she wasn't at the strip mall, she was online shopping, and if she wasn't online shopping, she was ordering every unnecessary thing known to man from the tele.

I walked into my closet and headed to the section I'd created a year prior just for my "gym clothing." It really was quite the joke, and my dear hubby made sure it was the punchline at each and every dinner party we've had for the past year. After one too many gin and tonics, he'd raise his glass and say, "Let's give a toast to the part of my wife's closet that hasn't seen her since she hung the clothes there! Her active wear section! This lovely lady has an active wear section, and isn't the slightest bit active!" Then he'd fold over in laughter. The first time he did it, he got a few to laugh with him, but now that everyone's used to the "joke," they attempt to ignore his tipsy comments to spare me. One time, he even tried to lead a tour through the house to my closet for a visual of the joke he seemed to find so funny. Here at last, I decided to give in, to relent, to give up my mornings of English muffins, espresso, and the early morning talk shows. I've decided to give my husband what he wants, so maybe I can get what I want...him back.

I left my precious monkey with my mum then headed over. I was actually nervous to walk into the exclusive gym, since I imagined there would be women there who looked like they stepped off the pages of the latest edition of Sports Illustrated or some fashion magazine, all there to work off the imaginary pounds they'd gained eating lettuce and drinking sparkling water. I decided that my best shot at not looking like the hog was to get to the gym by 8 A.M. I walked in with my coordinating black getup, looking like I was auditioning for an exercise video. It's pretty empty, so I'm pleased. I see the receptionist has had her coffee already as she greets me in a high pitched midday tone, "Good morning!"

"Hi, good morning. I'm a member here, but this is my first time, um working out, um here," I stammer.

"Oh, cool! Well, welcome! Wow, you have, like, the coolest accent. Are you from England or something?"

"Yes, I am. Do you have personal trainers? I really don't know what machines to use or how to use them."

"We sure do. And our personal trainers really are the best. I'll see who we have available now."

I watched her study the computer screen intensely and interrupted, "I'd really prefer a woman; I don't want any man looking at my rotund bum." I tried to joke.

"Let's see." She put her hand on her chin and stared at the screen like it was really brain science. "I'm sorry, but we only have one trainer available at the moment, but he's really great."

"Well, uh, I guess I will have to go with him then," I conceded.

"You won't be sorry, Ms. Alexander. Peter really is one of the coolest, and his workout plan is really good for women "

"Mrs. Alexander, dear." I felt the need to correct her for some reason.

Ignoring my statement about being Mrs. Alexander, the receptionist picked up the phone and called Peter over the loud speaker to the front desk. I stood there looking around the modern gym, noting the signs pointing towards the smoothie bar and the posters of beautiful people in their tight clothes showing their fit and toned bodies. I looked around and saw the early morning gym goers; they looked enthused to be there. Meanwhile, I just wanted to walk out of the gym, go home, and order myself a large pizza with all the toppings and whatever desert was offered as the special of the month.

"What's up, Amber?" I heard the deep, manly, southern-sounding voice before I saw the face.

The bubbly receptionist perked up and smiled, her face a bit redder than it was just moments before.

"Oh, Peter, this is your newest client, Mrs. Alexander." She made sure to emphasize the Mrs. This time around. I looked at her with a slight smirk then turned my attention to Peter. I couldn't help but turn a few shades of red myself as I felt a warmness come over me when I looked at him. He had on a sleeveless black gym shirt that hugged him ever so tightly. The bronze skin of his bicep glistened with just a hint of perspiration. I managed to make my way upwards of his arms to his face. He was the color of warm caramel, or that's what I saw when I looked at him. Yes, warm caramel as it covers vanilla ice cream. His eyes were round but slanted at the corners, giving him a cheery look. His lips were covered by a light mustache, and he wore a light, neatly-shaped beard. I noticed that he looked rather young, well, and younger than me. I easily surmised him as no more than 28. Peter wore his hair in neat cornrows that went straight back, giving him a slight rough edge. I was indeed in need of a fan.

When he spoke, it snapped me out of the mini caramel-induced fantasy I was about to embark on. Peter motioned for me to follow him, and I walked alongside him, nervous about the physical work I had ahead of me. Then, I thought of another holiday party with me as the butt of Corey's jokes, and I quickly remembered why I was at the gym.

"Nice to meet you, Mrs. Alexander," Peter finally said. "What made you decide that now's the time to get fit? Is it health reasons or just the desire to tone your body?"

I was somewhat taken aback by his question. I didn't quite know if I should be honest and tell him that my husband thinks I'm a fat cow and isn't attracted to me anymore.

"Just personal reasons; that's all."

"Well, you're in the right place. Don't worry, I'm gonna get you in the best shape of your life!" Peter promised with a slight smirk that made my heart do a little cardio. He had a cute country accent. I slightly giggled to myself, imagining that he'd ended his statement with a 'hee-haw.'

Over the next few weeks, I began an intense training with Peter. I'd get to the gym at 7 A.M., three days per week, and he'd have a vanilla banana whey protein smoothie waiting for me. We'd spend the first 15 minutes going over my workout plan and dietary concerns, since he had me on a low-carb, high-protein diet. I called this time with him breakfast with Peter.

I learned that he was originally from Frankfort, Kentucky, has a sister who just moved to New York, and a niece named, Casey, who he absolutely adores. He said he'd moved up north to go to college for sports medicine, and that after college, he decided not to move back to Kentucky but to settle in Connecticut and make personal training his profession. Peter's also a part-time bartender and promised to make me a tasty cocktail in the near future. He'd built a nice business for himself and loves what he does.

I'd been working hard; the regimen that Peter had me on worked wonders on my physique. Within four weeks, I was down 20 pounds, and as they say

I was certainly feeling myself. I started noticing Corey eyeing me at night as I dressed for bed; and while I'd been desperate for his attention before, I now wanted the attention of only one man: Peter.

"You're looking great! I see the definition coming along in those abs. I told you I would have you looking like a runway model soon enough Mr. Alexander's going to be fighting the men off!" He joked as he lightly placed his hand on my stomach.

"You're absolutely too much Peter!" I gushed.

"Peter! The way you say my name makes it sound so fancy," he teased.

"I'm hoping that my accent wears down to a more Western one sooner rather than later."

"Now that's one thing you don't want to lose. That British accent is so sexy," Peter complimented, looking at me in a way he never had before. There were a few seconds of silence between us before I excused myself to the gym shower.

"I'm going to go shower off; I must smell like a hog," I said.

"No, I like the smell of sweat from a good workout," Peter replied with a smile.

When I was leaving the gym, I saw Peter in the lobby talking to the receptionist. I kept walking, but he called out to me. As I watched him jog to catch up, I couldn't help but notice his cock swinging about in his shorts. I brought my eyes back up to meet his and smiled.

"Sara, I just wanted you to know you've been doing great." He stood there like he was trying to find stuff to say so I wouldn't leave yet.

"Peter, do you have some time today? I have some gym equipment at home that I need your opinion on." I don't even know why I said that, but then again, I did. I didn't have to pick up my son for a few hours, and it wasn't the maid's day to come. I just needed Peter's company.

He looked stunned as he rubbed his chin like he was thinking. "I don't have any more clients this morning, so I can come now if you'd like," he finally answered.

I headed out and walked to my car then waited for Peter to pull up behind me before I lead him out of the gym parking lot.

I noticed Peter's eyes widen as we walked in my house past the foyer. "Very nice house, Sara; your husband must do well."

"He works hard; I guess you can say. But he's working hard for the dollar, not hard to keep my heart."

"Well, I'm sorry to hear that. His loss, because you have a heart of gold from what I can tell." Peter was such a Southern gentleman.

I hadn't ever cheated on Corey; despite the numerous affairs I was well aware of. Now that I'd gotten myself in a shape worth showing a man naked, I didn't want to waste it on him. I unpinned my hair and let my lush red mane cascade down my back. I turned to Peter.

"Peter, tell me something. Do you find me attractive?" I asked as I pulled my t-shirt over my head. Before he could answer, I was pulling my pants down and stepping out of them.

"You're a very beautiful woman, Sara. Any man would be lucky to have you."

I could see Peter's answer, not from his face, but from the very large bulge in his sweats that moved upwards and slightly to the left. It looked like a large corn on the cob trying to make its way to the top of his pants, and oh how I loved corn.

I dropped to my knees in the foyer of the home I shared with my husband and child and pulled out the most delicious caramel-covered corn on the cob I'd ever seen. Peter was clean shaven, even his balls were bare. I looked up at him, standing there with his sweats around his knees before placing his big cock in my mouth. It was smooth, and I tried to swallow it. He ran his hands through my hair as he mumbled softly how it felt so good. I took his cock out and put his dark brown sacks into my mouth. They had drawn themselves tightly to his body, but I still sucked them vigorously yet gently. He moaned in ecstasy. When I put his cock back in my mouth and played with his sack concurrently, Peter pumped to match the speed and depth of the head I was giving. He moved faster, and I could taste his sweet pre-cum. I thought about all the smoothies he drinks and couldn't wait to taste his cum. His thrusting let me know he was on the brink of exploding, and before I could grab his shaft to give it a good jerk, his thick, sweet, hot liquid shot down my throat.

"Fuck! OH fuck! Suck it; swallow my cum!" Peter demanded as he jerked. His handsome face twisted in desire. I gave him about 30 seconds to recover, then I pulled his sweats back up, thanked him for his time they walked him to the door. Right before he got on the other side of the door, he stopped and turned towards me. "I guess you don't need help with some old gym equipment?"

"I had help with all the heavy equipment I needed a few minutes ago," I flirted as I licked my lips.

Peter simply smirked, and I closed the door, skipping in delight to the kitchen for a cold beverage.

I placed Rocko's treat in the fridge like I always did at my mum's house before I left for the gym.

"That gym really has been great for you, my dear. Not only have you lost weight, you're glowing! You look 10 years younger. I may have to start going to the gym myself," Mum said with a wink.

When I pulled back up to my house, I raced through the door, so I could shower quickly before Peter arrived. I knew I was wrong for carrying on in my home like a single woman, but I felt it was the least I could do after being humiliated for years by Corey. Just as I was drying off, I heard the doorbell ring. I wrapped the plush white towel around my breasts then headed down for my morning snack.

I opened the front door and dropped my towel as Peter walked in. He backed me into the house with his kiss, and I could feel the heat radiating from his body through his clothes onto my naked flesh. He groped my breasts aggressively, then I turned to lead him into the kitchen. While heading in the kitchen's direction, he slapped me on the bum so hard, I was sure his hand print was imprinted across my right cheek. I felt guilty for a moment as I reminisced on the days when Corey would do the same. But whatever bit of guilt I felt dissipated as soon as we walked into the kitchen, and Peter bent me over the island and knelt behind me.

His tongue plunged deep into my cave, and my juices felt like hot lava pouring down my thigh. My legs trembled as he worked my clitoris with both his finger and tongue simultaneously. Peter's tongue felt better than any vibrator I'd ever used. He had full control of its motion, rotating his tongue against my clit at speeds I didn't know were humanly possible. Corey hadn't been able to make me cum from oral, not even once during our entire marriage.

I felt the explosion building up, and I silently prayed that Peter wouldn't stop until I came. He didn't fail. I came with such a guttural sound that I barely recognized my own voice. When I stopped shaking, Peter helped me steady myself. I wiped his mouth with my tongue then led him up the winding staircase to my bedroom. I felt him hesitate behind me before entering.

"Wait, I don't know about this. Your bed?" Peter raised his eyebrows.

"No, not my bed dear. Beds are boring; follow me." I kept walking until I reached the walk-in closet Corey and I shared then opened the door. Peter's eyes widened as he looked around and saw that the closet was arranged by color and clothing type. I walked over to the cabinet that housed Corey's large collection of ties. I opened it and grabbed one of his favorites, a wine-colored satin tie that he'd picked up in France at one of his favorite boutiques.

"Lay down, Peter," I ordered then began licking his neck.

He pulled his t-shirt over his head and removed his black sweatpants. He didn't have on any underwear, and his dick bounced with buoyancy as it stood at attention.

"No, you lay down. As a matter of fact, get on your fucking knees, Sara," he demanded.

My heart fluttered with excitement, and my pussy watered with anticipation. I got on my knees as naked as I came in the world.

"Spread your knees apart," Peter requested barely above a whisper. I widened my legs as he wished.

"Wider!" He demanded.

I complied. He slid his index finger from my clitoris to my opening and slowly stroked my button. "Ah…you're so wet, Sara," he told me in a heavy, breathy voice.

I heard him go into his sweatpants pocket then open a rubber. He grabbed my ankles and brought them together. Then, he grabbed Corey's favorite tie and tied them together. I wanted to protest but didn't. Peter stood and went to the closet and grabbed another tie then blindfolded me.

"Sara, is it me you want inside of you?"

Before I could answer, he entered me. I almost fell forward from his thrust.

"Yesses, Peter," I moaned as he made slow, long strokes in and out of me. The smacking sound from my juices with every thrust was like music to my ears. Peter reached around and put his index finger in my mouth. I sucked it like it was his dick. Peter's hands were all over me as he stroked in a tender yet aggressive way.

"You mean to tell me your husband isn't giving this pussy attention, Sara?" Peter asked between breaths.

I just moaned in return.

"Answer me!" Peter yelled as he banged me harder.

"Pooh, it feels so good, Peter! No, he's not."

"Damn, you feel good," he groaned and sped up. Peter moved his waist in all kinds of circles, making my insides feel something they hadn't in many years. My body shook; I was weak. It was like all of my nerves were standing on end. I screamed as spurts of liquid shot from my body and wet the carpet under me.

"There you go, Sara! Let it all out." Peter said through what sounded like clinched teeth. Then I heard him yelp with pleasure.

"Shit! Fuck! Ahhhh!" Peter stroked slowly, getting out any last fluid from his body. I fell forward just as he untied my ankles and lay there on my closet floor, watching Peter get dressed. I looked around my closet with a different feeling than I'd ever had before. I smiled to myself as I looked over at my exercise clothes hanging neatly. I thought to myself that at our next social gathering, instead of Corey leading the guests through my house to the closet, I'll be the one leading the tours. When I chuckled, Peter turned to me and asked, "What's so funny?"

"Life, my dear, life. I'm still hungry, though. How about some more of that breakfast?" I asked as I pulled Peter down to the floor for round two before it was time to get back to my reality.

In the End...

NINA LOVED NEW YORK CITY AROUND THE holidays, especially during Christmas season. She closed her eyes as the flight attendant gave instructions for takeoff. Jock squeezed her hand, interrupting her thoughts.

"You okay baby?" He whispered in her ear.

"Yes, I'm fine. I'm daydreaming about New Year in the city! I can't wait to get to the party. Shannon said it's supposed to be the charity event of the year; anyone who's somebody important in the city attends this event," Nina told a snoring Jock, who'd fallen asleep before the plane's wheels left the ground.

Nina couldn't wait to see Shannon; she hadn't seen her since she and Chaz moved from Kentucky to New York to expand the business five months ago.

Nina walked the streets of the newly gentrified Harlem, on her way to meet Shannon for lunch and shopping. She was amazed at the change her city, and more specifically, her hood, had gone through. She reached the soul food restaurant that she had heard was the go-to spot in Harlem and saw Shannon was already there waiting for her.

"Nina!" Shannon jumped up from her seat and embraced her I.

"Look at you! You look great sis; I miss you so much!" Shannon rambled.

"I miss you, too! It's so cold up here, I almost forgot how the winters in my city are."

"Yes, girl, and you know I'm a country girl. I and Alissa are missing that country heat. Chaz is used to it so he keeps telling me I'll get used to it, but I don't know."

Shannon is so country, Nina thought to herself.

After the waitress came to take their orders, they continued catching up.

"How is Chaz? I know he and Jock speak daily, at least by text, but we all miss him around the office. He kept us in tears with his crazy self," Nina asked, knowing she really missed the physical feeling Chaz gave her.

"He's good. He's been really busy getting the business off the ground, so I don't even see him like I did when we were at home in Kentucky. He's always got some meeting to attend or some potential business partner to entertain," Shannon explained as she sipped her iced tea.

Nina placed her hand on her chin absentmindedly. She wondered if Chaz was sharing that marvelous dick of his with anyone else during his busy business meetings.

"What?" Shannon asked, sensing that something was on Nina's mind.

"Oh nothing," She paused, the said, "Well. I mean this *is* New York, home of the super model and the super freak. You think Chaz is playing around?" Nina was asking more for herself than Shannon.

"Oh, Chaz? No way, girl! I think he's just really busy. You know how focused he is; that's what made me fall in love with him." Shannon grinned like a naïve schoolgirl.

After their food came out, Nina and Shannon ate their lunch and caught up on all that's happened in their lives over the past five months. Shannon told Nina that her brother was living just outside of the city in Connecticut, so she felt a little more grounded now that she had family not too far away. When they finished their meal, they made their way to the busy New York City subway then down to Midtown to look for dresses for the gala.

"I haven't been to Barney's in a while. I need my time there!' Nina exclaimed, thinking about all of the fabulous clothing she would buy.

"You're so lucky, Nina. With a body like yours, you can wear anything."

"You should talk. Look at you!" Nina complimented as she held up a black strapless crystal-covered mini-dress up to Shannon's chest. "This will look absolutely wonderful on you~ And Chaz won't be able to keep his eyes off of you."

Nina then thought about what she could pick out for herself so that Chaz's attention would be on her as well.

Mia walked into the house, her garment bag weighing her down. She's been feeling blue since she stopped seeing Corey. *Perhaps this party will bring me out of my funk,*" she thought to herself as she pulled the fiery-red long halter top dress from the bag. The slit was so high up the thigh, she wondered if Rob would oppose the dress. "He needs something to give him a jolt," Mia mumbled to herself as she pulled the dress on to model in her mirror. "Then again, never mind," Mia mused, shaking her head. She took the dress off and stood in the mirror, taking in her own naked body.

She thought about how Corey would touch and caress her all over, not leaving an inch missed with his kisses. Mia hugged herself, imagining Corey behind her, holding her and whispering how beautiful she was in her ear. She closed her eyes and reminisced on how warm his bare chest felt against her back and how good he smelled, even at the end of a long work day.

"Mommy, what you doing?" Mia's fantasy was interrupted by her son's entry into her bedroom.

"Just trying on a dress for a big party I'm going to with your daddy." Mia poked at her son, causing him to hold his belly and giggle.

Summer hung up the phone and punched in the date and time for the order Mr. Stan Watford placed. This was the second year in a row that he'd asked her to be his guest at this stuffy ass charity dinner. Summer thought about all the money they spent to have the annual gala at a swanky hotel and turned her mouth down when she thought about how the food was always less than appetizing.

Mr. Watford was big in the construction business and had been investing a lot of money in all of the new properties popping up all over Brooklyn and Harlem. And while he came from old money, he never found his heart in old money women. Stan Watford liked his women with a little color and a lot of flavor. When she arrived to events on his arm, Summer could see the look in the eyes of the wives of some of Mr. Watford's business partners. The men slobbered out of the sides of their mouths, patting there little pudgiest down as they fidgeted in their seats. Their wives' eyes squinted with crooked downturned smiles upon their newly Restylane injected lips as they whispered to each other. They had to know their husbands used the service, too; Stan just didn't have a wife to hide it from.

He'd talk to Summer at dinner before sticking his dick in her, then go over his life. He'd done the wife and family thing in his early days. But by 50, he wanted to be free to fuck and get sucked at will without any attachments, because as he rationalized, "Relationships are overrated. Don't you think, Summer?" To which Summer nodded and smile, telling Stan whatever he wanted to hear. After all, that's what he was paying for. Not her real opinion.

Summer went online and ordered the most expensive dress she could find: A black Chanel cocktail dress. It wasn't too short, because she still wanted to look classy on this wealthy man's arm, but it was short enough to catch the attention of all the wealthy men in the room. Summer always remembered that she would be in the company of several new potential high-paying clients. The thought alone of green, her favorite color, turned her on more than the touch of any man.

"Sara! Sara! Where's my red tie with the small green trees on it?"

Sara could envision Corey running around the room in a frenzy, searching for the tie he always wore for every holiday event. He considered it his lucky tie as he had closed many a merger wearing it.

She held in her laughter as she yelled back, "I have no idea what you did with that tie! Why don't you just buy another?" A smile crept onto her face as she thought about the last time she'd seen that tie. Or rather felt it. Peter had used it to tie her wrists together as he rammed her from behind.

Sara went to her part of the closet and held up a fiery red dress to her neck. She'd been dying to wear it ever since Corey bought it a few years earlier. She actually believed he bought it as a way of teasing and taunting her, never truly believing that she'd ever be able to fit into the size six dress. It hit just above the knee with a nice, plunging neckline that showed off her natural double D breasts. Sara twirled, feeling more confident in her body than she had in years.

"What the hell are you doing?" Corey asked in an accusatory tone.

"What does it look like I'm doing? I'm modeling my dress, trying to see if it looks good enough for the charity ball."

"It's a little short, don't you think? You're not some young chap there, Sara."

"I'm only 32- years-old, Corey! I know I'm not the youngest horse in the stable, but I am entitled to look good, too, you know."

Corey huffed and retreated to his part of the closet, rummaging through like a mad man in search of that silly tie.

Sara rolled her eyes but laughed hysterically inside as she thought to herself *Ah, dear Corey, that fucking tie went in the trash, just like our so-called marriage.*

She didn't feel an ounce of pity as she watched him tear through the clothes like a maniac. Sara gently placed a hand on his shoulder and asked, "Love, did you find it yet?"

Rob was excited that he'd received an invitation to one of the biggest annual charity events hosted in New York City. This invitation cemented his place in the real estate industry, lining him up with the biggest names in construction and development.

I really have to make a good impression, he thought to himself as he admired his physique in the mirror. Rob curled his arm and felt his bicep, satisfied at how hard it felt. He flexed his pecs, one at a time, and his mind drifted back to his last time with Summer. Her succulent lips nibbling his nipple. He spent so much time thinking about her and what she did to his body. *Summer truly knows how to make a man feel like a man,* he thought. He was so caught up in his thoughts that he didn't even hear Mia enter the bedroom.

"Is that a banana in them boxers, or are you happy to see me?" She asked, wrapping her arms around his waist.

Rob, still lost in thought, quickly moved Mia's arms from around his waist. "When'd you get home?" He grabbed his t-shirt and pulled it over his head.

"I just got in. I thought I'd come home early so we could spend a little time together before we have to get the baby.

"Is everything okay? I walk in and see you with a dick harder than I've seen in a minute, and you act like I interrupted you. Should I leave?" Mia asked sarcastically.

"No. I just wasn't expecting you. I was actually just thinking about you," Rob lied. His dick had since deflated with Mia's interruption, but he figured he could think of Summer and give Mia the best 10 minutes she's had in a while.

Rob leaned in, closing his eyes as soon as his lips touched his wife. He pictured Summer in a black lace negligee with the crotch cut out. The thought made him push Mia on the bed and push her pencil skirt up to her waist. Stroking his dick, he thought about how delicious Summer tasted. He ripped the pantyhose off of his wife and pulled her panties down in one swift motion. He pushed himself inside of her and pounded, although she had yet to get as wet as he liked it. Rob pulled out and turned Mia over, figuring he'd be able to focus more on her ass since it was close in size to Summer's. He made his way back in once Mia was on her stomach and pumped her in a frenzy. His body was with Mia, but his mind was with Summer. He imagined Summer's face turning around to look back at him with pure ecstasy in her blue-gray eyes. Hearing Mia's faint moans were enough to make him cum, although not like the moans of Summer.

Recognizing it was his wife's pussy and not Summer's, he pulled out and came on her ass. Once he finished, he came back to his senses, trying to catch his breath as he sat on the side of the bed panting. Mia lay there, waiting for Rob to wipe her ass off like he usually did.

"Uh hello?! Can you grab a towel and wipe my ass?" When he didn't reply, she yelled, "You know what?! Never mind!" Mia huffed as she got up from the bed, trying not to get any of Rob's juices on the comforter. She made her way to the bathroom, which was located in their bedroom and got herself together.

Rob felt like he'd just fucked his wife like she was prostitute, and for the first time, guilt plagued him. "Damn, I'm starting to fuck up," he mumbled.

He knew that the time was coming when he would either stop seeing Summer or add some of the other girls on her roster to the menu. He had no intention of giving up the outside sex that he was becoming dependent on to keep him happily married.

He looked at Mia, who had her head cocked to one side, watching him curiously from the doorway, and decided to change the subject of his mind.

"Aye, honey, you got your dress for the gala?"

Showtime

To be on the invite list to one of the most coveted charity events held annually in New York City was an enviable position. Celebrities and socialites alike, who had nothing to do with the construction industry, bought their way into the gala just to rub noses with the who's who of the most elite of New York's social scene. This year was no different, but the gala being held on New Year's Eve was even better because it was on a Saturday for 2016, and the guests didn't have to deal with the casual business crowd that perused outside, trying to get a peek of the guests going in.

Rob decided to go all out for this event. There was no way he was pulling up in a car to this fancy hotel when he knew it was a red carpet event. He looked over at Mia; she was staring out of the window of their classic black limo. He liked that she put a little extra effort into her look for the night. She'd decided to do something different and cut her shoulder-length hair into a cut reminiscent of the classic Halle Berry 'do. Rob admired the slit of her satin black gown that showed just enough thigh through her sheer black pantyhose. Her ample cleavage was on display, classy enough to show that she was working with more than plenty to make any man lust after her.

"Penny for your thoughts," Rob broke their silence, hoping Mia was in the mood for a conversation. *The black mink looks so good against her skin,* Rob thought as she turned to face him. Mia smiled faintly.

"I was just admiring the city. I'm here every day for work, but I don't think I truly appreciate the beauty of it when I'm rushing to and from work," Mia lied. The limo had just passed the coffee shop where she and Corey had her first unofficial date. She longed for his voice, for his touch, and for the look in his eyes when he saw her. Rob didn't give her that desire any more, and he hadn't in a long time.

The limo pulled to the front of the swanky hotel, and Mia looked at Rob with a fake smile plastered on her face. The limo driver got out to open the door on Rob's side. After he got out, he put his hand out to help Mia out of the car. "It's show time, baby," Rob told her. When they both stepped out of the car, they were bombarded with f light from the numerous cameras flashing from the sidelines of the red carpet.

"I need to check my coat," Mia said to Rob as they entered the foyer of the hotel.

"Madam, the coat check is downstairs, right outside of the Templeton Ballroom for tonight's gala," a bald, middle-aged African American man replied, tilting his head in the direction the fanciest dressed people were going in. Mia nodded her thank you and lifted her chin, deciding to walk like those in her company. She took a flute of champagne from one of the waiters outside the ballroom. After Rob grabbed their table setting card and noted their table, they entered the ballroom. It was grander than he imagined, and he was surprised to hear Mia softly gasp. He saw her clench the diamond necklace he's purchased for their fifth wedding anniversary. The shocked look on her face made him proud that he was able to take her to such an event. Rob smiled and placed his hand on the small of her back, nudging her further inside the hall. When he noticed she seemed stuck, he whispered in her ear, "Honey don't act like you're not used to anything. We can't just stand here." He teased.

Mia thought she would faint right where she stood. There he was, in all of his fine chocolate-y glory. Corey. There in deep conversation with an older white- haired man at his table. He laughed at something the man said, but Mia knew it was a fake chuckle. She knew that his eyes got small when he was really tickled about something. Her heart fluttered, and without provocation, her nipples hardened. When she looked to his right and saw her, it was like a man's erection that deflates when he's turned off. There was a woman, who Mia presumed to be his wife. She looked absolutely uninterested as she flagged down the waiter and grabbed another flute of champagne. Mia was unsure of where she was for a split second until she heard Rob in her ear. His hand rested on her back, and she quickly followed his lead, praying they weren't sitting in any of the empty seats at Corey's table.

She heard Rob's "Here we are." Mia was relieved that it wasn't at Corey's table, but it surely wasn't far enough.

Of all the places, of all the tables in this large ass hall, why? Mia thought to herself nervously. Her stomach wouldn't allow her to eat any of the delicious-looking hors d'oeuvres offered by the help.

"These little lamb chops are damn good! Why aren't you eating? You'd better take advantage of this; you know we don't get invited to these types of events every day," Rob suggested and leaned in.

"I'm really not hungry, but I'll take another drink. I need something stronger than that Champagne. Can you go get me something from the bar?" Mia just needed a few moments to herself to collect her nerves.

"Okay, baby. I see you *do* need something strong. I'll surprise you." Rob got up and disappeared into the growing crowd of guests making their way into the hall. Mia refused to look in Corey's direction. She thought if she didn't look over, they wouldn't make eye contact and therefore, he wouldn't see her. But she didn't have to look over, because she felt his presence before she saw him. Her skin was quickly covered in chill bumps as she felt his fingertips move across the top of her back, just below her hairline. Reflexively, she closed her eyes, not caring about her surroundings.

Nina felt so excited to be in New York again. Since she'd been home, she shopped, ate at the restaurants she'd missed, and even did a little clubbing with some of her childhood friends. Jock and Chaz met up and went to a bar, but Nina had yet to see him.

She and Jock walked arm -in-arm into the ballroom, looking like money. Jock looked like the tuxedo company paid him to wear their design. His physique popped under the well-made suit. Nina wore her red sequined gown that fit like a glove and looked like she stepped off the page of a top fashion magazine. Her jet black hair was parted straight down the middle into a sleek bob that rested just under her chin. She painted her pursed lips a candy red that looked good against her caramel skin.

Nina scanned the room, wondering where Shannon and Chaz were. "You heard from Chaz? Are they here yet?" She asked Jock, trying not to sound too eager. "Yes, they're here somewhere. Chaz mentioned earlier that Shannon's brother, Pete, is here bartending tonight; you remember him, right?"

"Of course. He's a nice young man," Nina said out loud, but she thought to herself, *Hell yes, I remember Pete. Who could forget his fine ass?*

"We're at table nine," Jock announced, leading Nina to the table. As they approached, she saw there was already a couple there. The woman was seated, and her date, a fine dark-skinned man from what she could see, standing close behind her. Nina looked at the woman with a smile, but she seemed embarrassed for some reason. Her flushed cheeks didn't go unnoticed.

"Hi, I'm Nina, and this is my husband, Jock," Nina greeted, extending her hand to the beautiful woman.

"I'm Mia. My husband, Rob, went to the bar to grab a cocktail for me," Mia offered.

"I'm Corey Alexander. I just stopped by the table when I saw Mia; we did some business together in the past." He extended his hand to Jock.

"Are you in construction?" Jock asked.

"No. I'm in investment banking. I don't like to get my hands dirty with labor; I only like to get them dirty with money," Corey joked.

"Well, nice meeting you. Perhaps we can talk business some more tonight before the gala ends," Jock said as he turned his attention to his cellphone.

"Very well. Mia, it was great seeing you again." Corey nodded to Jock then made his way back to his table.

The exchange seemed a little more intimate to Nina than just old business friends. Nina watched Mia's eyes as she watched Corey go back to his table. She also noticed the woman sitting at the table locking eyes with Mia.

Seems like this is going to be an interesting night, Nina thought as she accepted the Champagne being offered to her. She raised her glass to Mia and nodded.

Rob felt important in the presence of all these people with money. He ordered his wife's drink then pulled out his wallet to tip the bartender a few dollars.

"You still got my card in there?" He heard her soft voice from behind as he took in her sweet scent, he felt the heat from her breath on his neck. Rob's dick grew hard instantly. He quickly turned around and looked over her shoulder to the table he shared with his wife. He wanted to make sure she wasn't watching him. She wasn't; instead, she was engaged in conversation with another couple who'd joined their table.

"Of course, I still have your card," Rob replied seductively, feeling turned on by the beautiful summer. He eyed her from head to toe. Her blond hair had been straightened but not so straight that it didn't have body; it had a slight large wave. The mini black cocktail dress clung to her small but voluptuous frame. Her lips were painted dark, a deep maroon that contrasted against her light skin. A sexy coy smile spread across her lips, and just then, an older white gentleman slid up close to her.

"Summer, there you are my dear. Did you get your drink?" He asked, placing a kiss on the nape of her neck while eyeing Rob.

"I was just about to order it, love," Summer replied as she quickly eyed Rob then made her way past him to the space next to him at the bar. Rob felt something similar to hunger pangs. His body needed to be on top of Summer in a bad way.

As he made his way back to the table with his wife's drink, all he could think of was taking Summer in the nearest bathroom and lifting her little black dress up around her waist. He didn't care how much it cost him for such an impromptu taste. It was a hunger he intended to satisfy before the gala's end.

Sara watched her husband's interaction with the pretty woman a few tables away. The way the woman closed her eyes told her that she knew him in the most private of ways. Sara remembered a time when Corey's fingertips did the same for her.

Corey locked eyes with Sara as he made his way back to the table. He knew she'd just witnessed his interaction with Mia. He'd tried to be as inconspicuous as possible, but he couldn't resist feeling the softness of Mia's skin on his fingertips. It was a feeling he missed immensely.

He'd seen saw Mia shortly after she entered the room. *How did she think she would go unnoticed?* Corey thought when he saw her. Every man within eye reach noticed the breath of fresh air that had breezed into the large hall. He'd tried to conceal his excitement, because Mia looked more beautiful than ever, her new haircut showing off more of her beautiful face than he thought possible. *So that's him? The husband. Ha,* Corey thought to himself that Mia could do better. He thought she should be married to a man a little more polished, someone like him, he mused.

"So, I see you have a friend here," Sara mentioned between sips of Champagne. Corey was hoping that she'd save this argument for home, or at least for the car ride home.

"Yes. Ah, we did business together a few months ago. Her firm and mine," he explained.

"I bet," Sara mused as she flagged down the waiter for more champagne and hors d'oeuvres.

Sara didn't really care much about what Corey was up to these days. In fact, she wanted him to be more occupied by his outside activities, because he'd been a bit clingy as of late. Peter kept Sara's libido more than satisfied, so Corey's touch had become less than desired, an annoyance even.

"This Champagne really is quite weak. I'm going to go to the bar. You can go back over and keep your business associate company while I'm gone." She paused. "Oh... whelp, it looks like her date's back," Sara quipped snidely in a low voice so none of the other table guests could hear. She got up, stumbling a bit but steadying herself on the back of Corey's chair.

As Sara headed to the bar, Corey took in his wife. She looked pretty damn good, better than he had seen her in years. Her ass seemed to have gotten bigger; not in the sense of fat but more firm. The red dress fit her form and showed her shape in a way that made Corey slightly jealous as he noticed the eyes of other men on her.

Sara spotted him handing a drink to the pretty girl who was sitting at Sara's table with an older gentleman. He gave the woman a smile that she recognized as flirtatious. Instantly, she became hot all over as a small amount of anger took over her body. It was one thing for Corey to play her for a fool in her face, but she wouldn't have her lover disregarding her feelings, too.

"Fancy seeing you here!" Sara interrupted Peter as he made eyes with Summer, right before Summer's date guided her away from the bar.

"Wow. What are you doing here?" Peter responded, his voice full of surprise and shame.

"I would ask you the same thing, but I see what you're doing. I'm with the lump of coal over there." Sara nodded her head in the direction of her table.

Peter looked through the crowd in the direction of Sara's nod. He saw a table full of guests but recognized her husband from the photos he'd seen at her house during their rendezvous. He gave her a sly smile.

"There he is, in the flesh. Let me make you a stiff drink, although I wish I could give you something else stiff right now. You look absolutely fuckable in that dress; I'd love to take it off of you," Peter told her. Her face became as red as her dress.

"Well bartender, give me something hard and stiff. You know how I like it."

Chaz and Shannon were working the crowd. He had a natural energy that allowed him to finesse the support of many investors. Jock made things happen with architectural design, and Chaz had the gift of gab that brought Jock's ideas to life. Together, they made a lot of money. Aside from making money, Chaz actually enjoyed his friendship with Jock; they were like Ying and Yang, complimenting each other with their differences and balancing each other out.

Chaz had wondered about Nina since he left. He'd casually ask about her via Jock or Shannon but didn't probe too much as to not raise suspicion about his inquiry. He often thought back to some of the sex he had with her, curious if she'd taken up with any other men in his absence to quench her sexual thirst. He shook his head to himself as he pictured Nina spread eagle across his desk in the office back in Kentucky. He loved Shannon more than most things, but sex with her held no candle to the sex he'd had with Nina.

He spotted her, and their eyes met. For a brief moment, Chaz felt as if the room was emptied, leaving just Nina and himself. Her smile made him blush. He was brought back to reality by the sound of Shannon's voice.

"Look baby, there they go." Shannon pointed to the table that was almost filled with other people, leaving just their two empty seats.

Chaz had always thought that Nina was a beautiful woman, but there was also an edge of sex that oozed from her aura that just turned him on.

"Well, well my favorite couple!" Jock stood up and embraced Shannon. "You look fabulous, Shannon; I see the city life agrees with a country girl like you." Jock stood back and looked Shannon over like she was on display. She did a little twirl, feeling herself, grateful for the compliment Jock had given her. Chaz made his way over to Nina, who was standing there, awaiting the feel of his arms around her.

"Chaz, you look wonderful. We miss you down in the dirty." Nina playfully hit his arm.

"You know this is home to me. I miss Kentucky, but I must say, it feels good to be home." Chaz felt himself getting turned on by the sight of Nina, so he made his way over to his seat. Nina began making introductions, ensuring that everyone knew each other's names. She also realized that the angle she was sitting at was a prime location to reach Chaz's legs under the table.

As everyone made small talk, Nina indulged in the free expensive tasting Champagne, all while imagining crawling under the table, unzipping his pants, and placing Chaz in her mouth.

Summer

Summer watched Rob and the woman she presumed to be his wife. *She's cute enough, I guess. Not what I would consider gorgeous or really oozing sex appeal. I guess that's why he's using my service. These women need to get it together, and keep their men happy.* She turned her mouth down at the thought.

"Do you know those people?" Stan asked and leaned closer to Summer, slightly annoyed that she seemed preoccupied when he was paying for her time and attention.

"I'm sorry, Stan. No, I don't know them. The woman just reminds me of an aunt of mine. A dear aunt who I haven't seen in years," Summer fibbed.

"Must be your aunt in her younger years. That beautiful woman doesn't look like anyone's aunt tonight, let alone yours," Stan replied in a snarky tone then turned his attention back to the conversation about money going on at the table. He'd deal with Summer in a different way later, and perhaps lessen her tip since she wasn't on her best behavior tonight.

Summer really didn't ever concern herself with the personal lives of her clients. As long as they could pay her, she figured their reasoning for paying for pussy was none of her business. Rob, on the other hand, wasn't like most of her clients. She liked him in a friendship kind of way. Not that she would fuck him for free – as it always boiled down to the dollar – but she would give him the time of day to talk since he seems kind of bright. Even though she tried to keep her attention at the table she shared with Stan, inevitably Summer and Rob's eyes met. When she saw Rob excuse himself from the table, she waited a few minutes and decided to do the same.

Just as she expected, Rob was waiting close to the entrance of the restrooms.

"I was hoping you'd come out here," he said, not wasting a moment. She watched him stick his head in the men's room quickly. Then, Rob grabbed Summer by the hand and quickly pulled her into the men's room and into a stall, which, fortunately, smelled as if it was just cleaned.

"Just bill me," Rob whispered as he placed kisses up Summer's neck while lifting her short black dress. She opened her legs wide, welcoming the touch from his fingers as he probed her damp and waiting vagina. Summer always kept protection on her and slid a condom from her garter belt. Rob unbuckled his pants, and he let them fall to his ankles like he wasn't in a public bathroom, at a charity event with his wife and potential business partners in a room just a few feet away. Rob nervously tried opening the condom wrapper. A When Summer noticing his angst, she took it, opened it, and guided it down his shaft. He shivered slightly as if he was going to cum by the feel of her touch alone. Summer propped her legs up on one wall of the stall, her back against the opposite wall. Rob moved her thin panties over to the side and slid in. The feeling of her warm walls overtook him, and Rob felt like he was at home. At home inside of her. He moved slowly at first, savoring the feeling of her wetness surrounding him. Summer couldn't help but feel turned on; Rob felt so good that she started moaning. He instinctively covered her mouth, not only because he didn't want to be caught, but because her moans turned him on so much, and he wanted to keep from exploding as long as he could. Rob made long, deep strokes inside of Summer then picked up speed with his cum making its way to the top of his dick. He pumped one last time and had to stifle his grunt as he came. He heard the water running just as the last bit of cum left his dick. Rob stood there, frozen, holding Summer's body in the air with her legs wrapped around his waist until he heard the footsteps leave the bathroom. He let her down slowly and gently then stuck his tongue into her mouth kissing, her like he'd never see her again. He peeked out of the stall to make sure the coast was clear then left. Summer made her way out of the stall a few minutes after she did and headed back to the gala.

"Bathroom crowded?" Mia asked Rob as he returned to his seat at the table.

They were just making a speech about how much building up the more urban areas is going to benefit more than just the occupants."

"Yes, and I don't think that cocktail I had agreed with me. Messed with my stomach a little," Rob lied as he patted his stomach. Mia really didn't care; she was just trying to make small talk. He could've been gone for the rest of the event for all she cared. His absence from the table gave Mia ample time to look over and watch Corey. She could tell from where she sat that Sara felt similarly; she seemed quite

Uninterested in what Corey was saying as he was so engaged in conversation with the people at his table.

Mia decided that she needed a few minutes away from the table herself. She was starting to feel overwhelmed, and the room seemed to be closing in on her. Everyone else at the table seemed so happy with their lives;

meanwhile, she was denying herself the one thing that seemed to bring her a sense of satisfaction: Corey.

"Honey, excuse me. I'll be right back," Mia said to Rob, who was now more relaxed than she'd had seen him in days.

"Sure baby," he replied, getting up from his chair just a little as Mia made her way away from their seats. He watched his wife, her switch effortless as she maneuvered her way through the hall.

She still looks good, Rob thought to himself. Although no matter how good Mia looked, it wasn't enough to put a halt on the craving he had for a taste of Summer.

Mia

Mia stepped outside and felt the blast of cold air immediately. She wasn't thinking of her fur or the weather when she decided to step out of the event for a few minutes. She just needed time to collect her thoughts without all the noise of random conversations going on at her table and around the large ballroom.

"Fancy finding you out here." Corey crept up behind her. He'd seen her leaving and followed her out, thinking he may not have another opportunity to see her in person again. He'd sat in the café every morning for the past week, hoping and waiting to see her just so he could ask her why she stopped seeing him. Mia turned around and smiled in relief at seeing Corey's face.

"I just came out for some air. It seemed to be a bit stuffy inside," Mia explained, folding her arms and rubbing them to try to warm herself up.

"Listen, Mia; I'd really like to talk to you. You don't know how much I've missed you," Corey pleaded his case. Although she was excited to hear him say that, she didn't want him to know how much she'd missed him, too.

"Corey, this is not the time nor place for this conversation." Mia had her head down, trying to avoid eye contact with the man who melted her inside and out.

"My driver's got my limo waiting just ahead. Come, sit in here with me for a few minutes. Five minutes of your time, Mia, that's all. Just give me five minutes," Corey pleaded. He ushered Mia to the waiting limousine, not waiting for her to answer. His driver held the door open and watched his employer and a female guest who was not his wife climb in. The driver smirked as he closed the door. Corey wasn't the first of his employers to have used that backseat for what some would consider unorthodox meetings.

Mia sat facing him. Her nipples hardened, and the little mound of flesh between her thighs began to pulsate. Corey didn't speak; it was as if he knew that Mia needed to be touched. By him.

He traced the lining of her face with his fingertips. "I don't know if I've ever been this captivated by a woman. You're absolutely exquisite," Corey complimented as his fingertips landed on her lips. He tilted Mia's chin toward him and tasted her lips. She didn't protest. She kissed him back softly at first, but then she kissed him hungrily, feeding on the meal she'd been missing. Mia climbed on Corey's lap until she was straddling him face-to-face. She paused to guide her dress up around her waist, and Corey clumsily unbuckled his pants in a rush. Mia mounted his big, waiting dick and sighed with relief and pleasure at the feeling. Corey found Mia's breast and cupped the right one with his hand, while he sucked the left one greedily. She moved fast, jockeying his dick and reaching her orgasm quickly. "Oooh shit, Corey!" she moaned in his ear. Mia was weak and satiated, but Corey was determined to have his way. He grabbed her, one hand on her small waist and the other on her ample ass. Corey guided her frame in a fast pace to ensure every drop of his juice was released from his body. He felt himself Cumming, and Mia could feel that he was about to as well. She moved recklessly on his dick, helping him relieve his load inside her womb. When she knew Corey was empty, she climbed down from him. She pulled her dress down and turned to him.

"How do I look?" Mia asked, nervously smoothing down her hair.

"Like you've just been fucked good," Corey answered as he wiped some smudged lipstick from around her mouth.

"I have to get back," she said, rushing toward the limousine door.

Just as she stepped a foot on the ground, Corey grabbed her by the wrist. "I'm looking forward to making love to you, Mia."

She couldn't help but smile at Corey. She offered him a nod that reassured him that they would, indeed. Meet again as she hurried to the ladies' room to freshen up. Mia walked in the extravagant hotel feeling like a new woman. She certainly felt different than she did when she first got to the gala.

She freshened up and was putting on her lipstick when she saw a pretty younger woman watching her while she, too, applied makeup.

"I love that color, That deep red really suits you. It's so sexy!" the young woman complimented as if she was excited about something.

"Yes, I thought it'd be nice for tonight. I usually wouldn't ever wear such a bright color," Mia explained. She eyed the girl, who was not just pretty, but drop dead gorgeous. She was a little taller than average with pretty gray eyes and what looked like naturally blond hair, although you could tell she was black or at least had some black in her.

"Well, that's a shame. Beautiful woman like yourself should try that sexy red more often. I'm sure your husband would appreciate it," the young woman said then walked out of the ladies' room. Mia shook her head. The hell if she would take advice from a young girl on what her husband would appreciate. She looked at herself one more time, smoothing down her gown then made her way back to the table.

"I was just about to have someone check the ladies' room. You feeling okay?" Rob said as he got up to pull out Mia's chair.

"I feel great. Honey, listen they're playing our song!" Mia exclaimed, feeling invigorated. She grabbed Rob's hand and headed to the dance floor.

Sara

Sara played with the olive in her martini glass and watched Peter as he served the guests. *He's so beautiful. I can't believe I'm fucking him,*" Sara thought to herself. She had been sitting at the table, wondering when she would get to feel Peter again. She hardly noticed that Corey had left the table. Sara looked around the room, noting the individual faces. *Look at him. Rich, snobby bastard... Look at her, just as tired of her dear darlings' shit as I am.* Sara laughed out loud at the joke she'd told herself. Corey returned to the table just as Sara was getting up. She'd had enough of just watching Peter; she wanted to get up close and personal. The constant flow of Champagne mixed with the martini told Sara she should go see her man.

"Where are you off to?" Corey grabbed Sara by the elbow just as she walked away.

"I'm going to the same place you just came from, love," Sara mused, snatching her elbow away from his grip. Corey didn't care to track Sara's goings and comings. He just hoped she didn't embarrass him with her intoxication. He sat down and sipped the cognac waiting for him. Sara knew exactly what to order him, and it was just what he needed to top off the orgasm he'd just experienced with Mia. He watched her on the dance floor with her husband. As they danced slowly, her eyes met his, and she watched Corey over his shoulder with a smile.

Sara didn't know it, but Peter had been watching her since he found out she was there. He felt a bit of sadness for her when he saw how lonely she was in the company of her husband He didn't seem to pay her any attention, and Peter couldn't imagine treating a woman like Sara that way. He thought Corey was a fool for his behavior, and in a way, he was grateful for Corey's neglectful treatment of Sara since he'd benefited from it with tons of sex. She'd helped Peter fulfill fantasies he'd always had. He licked his lips as Sara made her way to him. He glanced at the clock, happy that he was entitled to a 15-minute break. After letting one of the other bartenders know he was going on break, he motioned for Sara to follow him.

Sara was so aroused at the sight of Peter. She was used to seeing him in sweats, and he looked so sexy in his tuxedo. Once they were in the hallway outside of the hall, Peter gave Sara a nod and look that said 'Just follow me.' He stopped at a door not too far outside of the hall. Sara saw waiters coming in and out of what seemed to be a revolving door as Champagne and appetizers flowed in and out continuously. She wondered where he was leading her. The other waiters seemed to pay her no attention as she walked into the busy kitchen area. Chefs yelled out demands and orders and screamed at the cooks for unknown reasons. Sara could smell the familiar, delicious scent of filet mignon being seared, salmon being poached, and chicken being braised. As appetizing as it smelled, she was only hungry for one thing at the moment.

Peter turned around to make sure Sara was close on his heels. He'd found the pantry he wanted and quickly looked around to see if anyone was paying attention. Everyone was moving fast, making sure things were on point for the important guests, so they didn't even notice Peter and the guest who'd just made their way through the large kitchen. When he opened the door, Sara felt the draft from the room. Peter didn't bother to turn on the light; as soon as the door closed, he grabbed Sara and kissed her deeply. He swirled his tongue around Sara's mouth, plunging so deeply that he could taste the alcohol she'd consumed earlier. Peter took his tongue out of her mouth and used it to trace down her neck to her breast. He opened his mouth and sucked on her right breast first, gripping the left one while he teasing her nipple with his tongue and finger simultaneously. He knew this always drove Sara crazy. She was so turned on that she lifted her gown and put one hand inside of her panties to play with herself and using the other hand to stroke Peter outside of his tuxedo pants. Feeling his bulge turned her on so much.

When Peter backed Sara into a wall, she flinched when she felt coldness of glass touch her back. The cold circles on her back let her know she was in a wine pantry, a chilled wine pantry. Peter had her so hot from the inside out that she couldn't feel just how cold the room actually was. He steadied her against the expensive bottles then removed her hand forcefully from her panties. He dropped to his knees and tasted her, licking the entire opening slowly at first; then he pushed his thick tongue inside of her to enjoy her taste. It didn't take Sara long to give him what he was waiting for as she stifled her moan and gave him her juices. She knew time was of the essence, but even as she panted, out of breath from the explosion she'd just experienced, she moved Peter around so that his back was now against the cold bottles. His dick was crammed in his pants and demanding freedom to get out. Sara squatted in front of Peter, in an unladylike way with her legs agape and her dress around her waist. A Then she took Peter deep into her throat. He didn't want to mess up her hair, even though he was used to having his hands all through it. Instead, he held on to the back of her head and threw his own head back. Sara sucked Peter's dick like she was going to get Champagne from it. Fondling his large, smooth, hairless balls, she licked them one at a time before putting them both in her mouth, sucking gently. Peter gasped with pleasure. Sara put his cock back in her mouth and sucked aggressively. He couldn't hold it in any longer and let her know. "I'm about to cum," he said just above a whisper.

Not a drop was spilled as Sara took every ounce of Peter down her throat. He shuddered, and his eyes rolled to the top of his head. As he felt the blood leaving his erection, he slowly removed himself out of Sara's unrelenting mouth. It was like she could suck it all night.

"We'd better get back; my break must be about over by now," Peter said as he helped Sara up from her squatted position in front of him. He put himself back in his pants. Although he couldn't see Sara because the room was dark, he reminded her, "Make sure your dress is down." He grabbed her hand and felt his way to the door.

"My goodness, it's quite chilly in here," Sara pointed out.

"Oh, you're just now feeling that?" Peter teased.

"What can I say, Peter? You had me hot."

When Sara entered the ballroom, she saw Corey sitting where she'd left him: at the table drinking and watching the same woman he'd been watching earlier. He was observing her on the dance floor as she danced with her man. She smirked as she approached him then bent down to his ear. "Let me guess, love. You were wondering where your beautiful wife was because you are ready to join those lovely couples on the dance floor."

Corey had been lost in his thoughts, thinking about how good Mia felt when she rode him in the limousine. He wondered if Mia enjoyed sex with her husband as much as she enjoyed it with him. *She couldn't,* he thought. Sara's voice jarred him back to the here and now.

"You know me so well," Corey lied. He grabbed his wife's hand and asked, "Shall we?" He nodded in the direction of the crowded dance floor. " We shall," Sara answered but not before she turned and met Peter's eyes. She winked at him then made her way to the floor with her husband.

Nina

Nina couldn't believe they were playing music you could actually dance to at such a swanky event. She wrapped her arms around Jock's neck and pecked him on the lips. The DJ had just slowed the music and "Beautiful" by Musiq Soulchild played thru the hall. Nina closed her eyes and lay her head on her husband's shoulders as he sang the words softly in her ear.

"*You're my baby, my lover, my lady. All night you make me want you. It drives me crazy. I feel like you were made just for me babe. Tell me if you feel the same way,*" Jock crooned softly. Nina had her eyes shut tightly, swaying smoothly to the rhythm and enjoying the feeling of Jock's heartbeat against hers.

As the music continued to play, her mind drifted back to Chaz. She tried to stay in the moment with Jock. He wasn't the most romantic man, so when she was awarded a romantic gesture on his part, she usually relished it. Nina opened her eyes, and when she looked over Jock's shoulder, she immediately found Chaz's eyes waiting for hers. His lips were moving as he sang along with the song: "*When you're not here, you don't know how much I miss you. The whole time on my mind, is how much I'm gonna get to make, you feel so good like you know I could.*"

Shannon's head rested, on his shoulder presumably lost in her own thoughts as her man mouthed the words to me. Nina watched his lips move until Jock swayed her body to a place where she could no longer see Chaz's face. Being within arm's length of Chaz, she found herself with a serious urge to reach out and touch him.

Jock and Nina returned to their table followed by Shannon and Chaz. Nina sipped her Champagne and watched Chaz's interactions with Shannon.

She was hoping he could read her thoughts, that he could tell how much she needed to feel his touch, how much she needed to feel his thick tongue and thick dick inside of her. Nina slipped a shoe off and stretched my leg out, hoping to reach his leg and not Shannon's. He smiled a sexy small smile when he felt her foot slowly make its way up his leg. She couldn't reach much further than his calf without becoming noticeable, so Nina slipped her foot back into the shoe, happy that she'd gotten his attention. She was becoming inpatient and looked around the room, trying to figure out how she could get a few minutes alone with him. That's all she needed. Just a dose to get her through her trip back home to Kentucky, somewhere to put her thoughts as she flew back home without him. Nina decided to be brave. *Fuck it. It's now or never,* she thought. She pulled her cellphone out of its sparkly designer wristlet. **2407** is what she texted Chaz with trembling fingers.

Nina then tapped Jock lightly on the hand and spoke when he turned to her, "Honey, I'm going to make my rounds, speak to some of the wives of the bigwigs. I'll be back."

She made her way over to Mrs. Rothstein, who smiled as Nina approached. "Nina darling, you look amazing! Have you had work done?" Judith Rothstein was so superficial, and her forehead didn't move an inch as she spoke.

"I haven't yet. I've been thinking of doing a little something with these lines around my mouth and maybe a little filler for my top lip. Can you believe they're thinning as I age?" She giggled, making the small talk Nina knew she loved.

"Well, I know the perfect doctor. You'll have to do it here in the city, though, not down there in that country. I don't know how you do it down there." She shook her head then went on. "There's nothing there. Anyway, Dr. Kaplan is on 5th Avenue, and he does everyone who's anyone. He's not bad on the eyes either. He'll have those lips plump in no time." Judith smiled with a knowing wink.

"Send me his info; I'll be sure to make an appointment," Nina told her then made her way through the crowd. She just needed to get through to the middle of the room where the crowd was full so she could get out of

Jock's sight easily for a few minutes. Once Nina got into the thick of it, she turned back to look at her table and see if Jock would be able to see her from where he sat. Once she couldn't see him, Nina strategically made her way through the crowd to the exit furthest away from their table. She was hoping that Chaz was watching her every step and that he took her up on her offer. As soon as she stepped out of the hall, she exhaled. For every ounce of nervousness she felt, Nina felt two ounces of desire, need, and desperation for the feel of Chaz. She walked through the hotel lobby and made her way to the elevator, hoping she'd gone unnoticed.

She got off the elevator, feeling like a fool as she slid her keycard in the door. Nina walked into the large suite she shared with her husband. "You have lost your damn mind," she mumbled to herself. She began to feel shame and guilt for having the nerve to even think about bringing her husband's best friend and business partner up to their room. She started thinking that perhaps she needed to make an appointment with a psychologist or therapist as soon as she returned to Kentucky. *Only a crazy person would even consider doing what I am*, Nina thought. She ran to the bathroom and looked at herself in the mirror. "Girl, get it together!" She commanded. She made her way to the door, determined to leave Chaz alone for good. When she opened the door, Nina came face-to -ace with him. He stood there for what seemed like forever but it was only a few seconds. She could tell he was reluctant to step into the room, but like Nina, he ignored his inner voice and stepped over the threshold. It didn't take anything but him entering the room.

Once the door closed behind him, Chaz grabbed Nina by the face and plunged his tongue into her mouth. His tongue tasted minty and delicious. His kisses moved down my neck in an intense manner. They were both hungry for each other, their hands traveling fast and in a frenzy, roaming each other's bodies. Nina lifted her dress, and Chaz slid her panties to the side as she unbuckled his pants. With her back against the wall, he picked her up, and Nina wrapped her legs around his waist. He pushed his boxers down to meet his pants, which were already gathered at his ankles and pushed himself in her already wet opening. You ever had an itch you couldn't get to, but when you did, it felt so good to be scratched? Nina felt a sense of relief and sighed with pleasure as Chaz moved himself inside of her while sucking on her breast. She tasted his face, licking his forehead, eyelids, even his hair was in her mouth. Any bit of him that she could get, Nina was willing to take. Chaz grunted and moaned, sounding both pleasured and pained. When he started pumping faster, she knew her ride was almost over. Nina appreciated every second and tried to store the feeling of each stroke for her memory's sake.

"Niiinaaa," Chaz groaned. His warm body fluid entered and filled Nina up. When he finished, he let her down easily. His eyes never met hers, and Nina knew exactly how he felt, sharing the poignant reality of their situation. She watched Chaz pull up then zip his pants and walk to the door without saying a word. As the door closed behind him, Nina wondered if this was their last time.

She knew she had to get back to Jock. Nina had gotten what she wanted and more importantly, needed, from her trip to New York.

"Nina! There you are!" Jock met her at the entrance to the hall. "I was just about to come looking for you. Are you okay? You look flushed." Jock looked and sounded concerned.

"I'm fine. I just went to the ladies' room to splash some water on my face. I think I've had one too many glasses of the bubbly." Nina smiled, ready to enjoy the rest of the party.

Stan swirled his expensive cognac around in his glass and leaned forward. He had made his fortune off of his ability to read faces, body language and energy. It was the reason he was rich and single. He was able to discern the strategies to take in business easily, and he was able to read women well. "I don't have time for the bullshit these people have to deal with" he thought as he smirked to himself. Stan studied the people who were sitting just a few tables away. "Look at this one. Sweat still fresh on his forehead. I wonder how many rocks he got off with that guy's wife." Stan wondered. "This one here at this table's so caught up in his own shit that he's not even aware that his broad's screwing the bartender." Stan watched Corey and lifted his glass to Corey in a salute when their eyes met. "That's why I pay for my pleasure. Easy. I enjoy when I want no excuses, no BS, no drama. Hell you pay for it being married to a chick, and what's worse you're paying for the same snatch every time you have the need to release. The fuck. I can't see it." Stan chuckled out loud at his thoughts.

"What's so funny? Enlighten me." Summer said, paying Stan more attention that she had all evening. Stan was in no mood for Summer's concern after he could damn near smell the used latex emanating from under her short dress. Stan's lips formed a thin line before going up just slightly on the right side of his mouth. Stan leaned in to Summer's ear, careful not to let anyone else the table hear his plans.

"I was just thinking about what form of pleasurable punishment you would have tonight. Dear." Stan took another swig of his drink. He didn't want to get too inebriated knowing it would soon be his turn to make his way to the podium to give a speech at tonight's charity event. Summer's eyes widened at the thought of Stan's punishment. She knew he could be extremely rough and uniquely abrasive when it came to sex. She shuddered at the thought of what tonight's antics would be like. She was hoping he didn't have plans for "the collar". She hated when he put the collar on her and fastened her hands to it. It really made her feel powerless, but she knew that's exactly the feeling he wanted her to experience. The extra money she received during these acts was great but it always took her a few days to recover both physically and mentally from the act.

Stan looked around the large room and shook his head as he listened to the speaker who was at the podium ranting about poverty and the duty we have to help end it. "Look at Tom giving off his help the poor rhetoric." Stan thought. "The first impoverished person he should be helping is that clerk in his office he's screwing. There's so much money in this room and not one of these fuckers really care about charity or the poor. We're damn sure not going to end it by putting up more of the expensive real estate that we're planning to do." Stan offered a phony smile and once again lifted his almost empty glass to Tom as Tom ended his speech with an elaborate introduction about Stan and all he's done to help those living under the Federal Poverty Limit in the city. Stan rose to his feet and made his way to the stage as the ballroom gave him a raucous applause.

Stan stood at the podium and cleared his throat as he waited for the applause to settle down. He didn't care about what people did in their private lives. But he was bored and a little tired of the shenanigans. He decided at the last minute to change his speech a bit and give a slightly different message. "I'll wing it, what the heck." Stan thought as he looked over the posh crowd.

"Thank you. Thank you for that most generous welcome, and thank you Tom for that ostentatious introduction. It's great that this year's event is being held on New Year's Eve. An opportunity for us all to start afresh. How great is that? You know I come to this event every year, and events like this multiple times throughout the year. Yes, I'm a creature of habit. Don't get me wrong, I like the fact that we all have to donate a large amount of money to get a ticket to eat a meal prepared by these wonderful chefs here." Stan paused to allow the audience a moment to be humored.

"What I really love about these events is the fact that I get to bring a lovely lady of my choice, and I get to people watch. I know some of you in this room may have grown up impoverished like the people we are hoping to help tonight. My question to you is what are you as an individual doing to help those who may have grown up in the communities you were raised in. Are we all so caught up in our personal dalliances that we have forgotten to be appreciative for the successes we have obtained? Are we so caught up in the business of making more money that we can't even see those who sit next to us, those who sleep next to us? I challenge you all in this room, when you leave tonight's event to be more cognizant of the people in your lives. Remove yourself from your own personal concentrations and seek to be attentive to others. I know this may seem offhand to helping those in poverty, but charity does start at home. Can I have a Touché? "Stan heard random Touches' coming from the audience.

"You see, most of us may be wealthy according to our bank accounts. Yet poor in other ways, in lifeless relationships, living lives filled with secrecy. Now that you have money, are you all happy? I know this may sound cliché but I have a feeling that some of the poor that we're contributing to are happier than a lot of you sitting in this room." Stan could hear the gasps, and see random heads shaking. He knew that he struck a chord. The wealthy don't like to let on that their money isn't making them happy.

"Six degrees of separation. We've all heard that saying before. The idea that all people are six or less steps away from each other. That saying a friend of a friend is true and can be made to connect any two people in a maximum of six steps. Isn't that interesting? So as I sat here tonight and observed as I like to do, I realized that the theory is truer than I thought. I saw eyes widen as people made eye contact with others, I saw looks exchanged on knowing eyes of those who are supposed to be strangers. What I also realized is once again, this theory proves that we all, in our richest of social circles are still six people away from someone who is less fortunate. As I end this speech tonight, I again invite you to turn your inclination to those closest to you. Reexamine each other, understand that in order to help others on the outside you must first be able to see what's going on in own environment. Happy New Year to you all. Thank you." Stan said as he nodded and stepped away from the podium with applause. As he made his way to his table, he glanced over at the table with the couples who all seemed to be intertwined in a salacious assembly. Some eyes averted his, as a few looked at him with wonder. He looked at his own table and saw a similar looks of shame from the banker Corey. His wife on the other hand was way past drunk and despite her husband's presence, she couldn't keep her eyes off of the bartender. Summer, however had no shame on her face. He knew for her it was business as usual as she shot him a devious smile. Stan responded in turn with a wink knowing Summer and as cold as it was that December night, that she would be bringing the heat.

Other Titles by Mahogany Star

Where Secrets Lie
Where Secrets Lie Pt. 2

Coming Soon

Spring 2017 Summer's Heat
Summer 2017 Grown Ass-The I.S. McCord Bio

Summer's Heat Inc.

A Novel by Mahogany Star

Prologue

IT WAS A SCORCHING 100.5 DEGREES OUTSIDE that 20th day of July in 1991, so my mama decided to name me Summer. She says I caused her blood pressure to rise, her body to swell, and her libido to go into overdrive, so she knew I was going to be trouble. I was the last of three children, a baby girl in house of older brothers. My brother Rich was ten when I was born, Kareem was eight, and I was cared for like a precious new toy. I was spoiled, and treated as the prize, my golden hair, hazel eyes and bronzed skin standing out from my siblings, who bore my father's dark skin and dark hair. My father treated me like a princess, until I was ten. There was nothing I could ask for that he wouldn't see to it that I got, whether he had to beg, borrow or steal to get it.

We lived a relatively middle class life, in my father's childhood home a four-bedroom brownstone in Bedford Stuyvesant Brooklyn. My father was a Sanitation worker and my mother a Secretary at a Social Services office in Downtown Brooklyn. Every day I would sit on the stoop and wait for my Daddy to get home from work. He'd see me, and scoop me up in his muscular arms. Although he smelled of the day's work, I didn't mind, my daddy was so sweet he even made garbage smell good. He always seemed to have put in a hard's day work, but he never missed a chance to show me affection. My mother would watch us and smile, full of pride as she looked on from the kitchen window. I was the epitome of a daddy's girl; we were the prize in each other's eyes.

By the time I turned ten, my oldest brother Rich had finished his second year of college, and my brother Kareem had enlisted in the Marine Corps. So mama and I only had one man to relish our affections on. Most of my friends didn't come from two parent homes, and I'd take every chance I got, to make sure they knew how good my Daddy was to me. The Christmas before I turned ten, my father somehow managed to buy my mother a mink. I smiled rubbing my little fingers through the black soft fur. It felt so good. I was so enthralled by my mother's mink that I didn't notice my father standing behind me, till he tapped me on the shoulder. "Princess, oh Princess, this is for you!" I ripped shiny red wrapping off the box and threw the top off only to find an exact replica of my mama's fur, but smaller.

"Summer, don't just stand there with your mouth wide open, try it on!" I heard my mother say. My father took the mini mink out of the box and held it open for me to slide my arms in, just like he did for my mama. Those were the best years of my life. Unfortunately, there were only ten years like that…

ONE

MY BEST FRIEND KASHA WAS WALKING ME home from a sleepover at her house when we walked into a chaotic scene out in front of my house. My father stood on top of a pile of clothes, he was standing on my favorite purple top, while he held my mother up by the collar of her blouse.

"You stankin bitch! I should've known you were no good."

I heard my mother screaming, pleading as onlooker's watched from their windows and from the streets. Some nosey neighbors had even decided to get a front row view from their stoops.

My heart beat so fast I thought I would pee my pants. I ran over to my daddy's arm and pulled it, trying to get him to look at me.

"Daddy, daddy, please. Please don't hurt mama."

It took a few moments before he would even acknowledge me. He looked down at me with red blood shot eyes that I didn't recognize.

"Yo mama's a ho, and I ain't yo daddy!" He said as a single tear left his right eye, and he shoved my mother to the floor.

I ran to my mama's side, where she lay in a fetal position crying hysterically. My father went back into the house and began to throw more clothes out of the front window. I cried as I watched my beautiful mink fly into the air, tossed like yesterday's trash.

"Trish, get yo ass off my property and take your little red bastard with you." He ranted. I heard my neighbor, Ms. Paula shout up to the window, "now Joe you know that you didn't have to go there. That child ain't got nothing to do with what her mama did. She innocent Joe!"

My father wasn't interested; he slammed the window shut along with his heart.

I forgot my friend Kasha was there, watching me be discarded. She came over and touched my shoulder, but I was in no mood for her consolation.

"Go home Kasha, get out of here." I said just as nastily as I could.

I knew Kasha, was glad to have the satisfaction of watching my pride and joy Daddy disown me. The daddy I always bragged on.

I helped my mother up from the ground, and watched as a neighbor picked our belongings off the ground, and packed them in large black trash bags. I wiped my mother's tears and my own, as people watched us walk slowly from the tree lined block.

We had been staying with my grandmother in the projects, my mother's old room was still there. My grandmother had three bedrooms, but she rented out the third bedroom to whoever needed it at the moment. It was how she made what she called her number money. It was so hard for me at first. I called my father constantly, begging him to let me back into his life, but whenever he heard my voice on the other end of the phone he'd just hang up. I asked my mother what happened over and over but she never answered. She'd just look at me, and say "you'll understand when you get older". I refused to wait till I was older to understand why my Daddy had thrown me out on the curb. I questioned what had I done wrong.

One night I got up to get a glass of water and I heard my grandmother talking on the phone. At first I thought she was just doing her usual building gossip until I heard her mention my name.

"That po' chile. Summer aint deserve to see the only man she ever known as Daddy throw her and her mama on the street." She paused. "Well I told Trish, eleven years ago to stop messing around on that man. Um, hmm. Yeah, she was sleeping with some white man on the job I hear tell of it. That's why that chile look like that. How Trish and Joe black ass gone produce a blond haired child? That man was a fool from the git."

Then my grandmother laughed out loud.

"You know how he found out right? That bitch of a friend of hers Debbie. Yessir that bitch was trying to get with Joe and told him about Trish and ole boy." She paused to take a pull of her cigarette.

"No Trish aint beat that bitch ass, cause she know it's true. Hell everybody down there at that welfare office she works at knew she was carrying that man baby. That son of a bitch lived on Long Island with a wife and some kids. You think he wanted his wife to find out about the black bitch he got pregnant at work? He up and left that damn job right after she came off a maternity leave. She bought that picture of Summer and he saw his blond headed baby and flew his ass up out of that office. Hehehehe, yessir he did."

My grandmother laughed into the phone so heartily. I was frozen, I lost my thirst, my heart was broken and I understood my father's pain.

How could Joe not be my father? The man who played Santa every Christmas, the man who gave me a new twenty-dollar bill when I lost my first tooth? I dropped the glass of water letting the glass shatter like my heart. I screamed out loud, I didn't care, my mother came running from our bedroom and my grandmother even hung up the phone to come to my aid. I stood there in place as the water flowed nonstop from my eyes. My mother tried to comfort me by pulling me in and embracing me. She tilted my head towards her bosom and I cried uncontrollably, my grandmother just shook her head and went back to her room and closed the door.

I didn't say anything to my mother about what I'd heard. It was useless and I wasn't up for her lies anyway. It all made sense. I stood in the small bathroom and just stared at my reflection in the mirror. Grandmother was right, there was no way I was Joe Smith's child. I didn't have one feature of his, not one. I wondered how he could've been fooled for as long as he was. Maybe he knew and didn't care, but he didn't want others to know he had been made a fool of.

School was eventful; my friends now had something they considered over me. It didn't help that my gear began to look tattered and worn from the cheap ass detergent my mother had begun using. My brother Kareem sent my mother a little money home from the service when he could. But my mother couldn't seem to get it together. I knew she wasn't paying my grandmother that much rent money, but whenever I asked her for money for new clothes she always said "baby we don't have no money."

I would reason that she worked every day, but she always came back at me with "We're broke. That's it, now leave me alone!" Then she'd retreat to the bedroom and stay in there until she went to work the next day. I'd sit on the bench in front of the building and jump rope with my friends. One day I decided I had to see my father so I walked to my old house and rang the bell. My stomach did somersaults, until I heard a woman's voice say "I'll be right there!" I thought I would faint when my mother's old best friend Debbie stood in the doorway wearing one of my mother's old Asian style robes. "Well little Summer, what are you doing here?" Debbie said in a cunning tone.

"I'm here to see my father." I said as I pushed my way past her.

Debbie wasn't about to let that happen so she grabbed me by the arm, and when she did that I turned around and spit in her face. She didn't hesitate to slap the shit out of me, the sting causing me to pause holding the side of my face for a few moments. Yet that didn't stop me, I threw myself at her and gave her all the fight my ten-year-old little body could. We rolled in the foyer until Joe came down the stairs to tear us apart. I made sure my mother's silky robe was ripped from her body.

"What the fuck is going on down here?" My father yelled as he handled Debbie roughly demanding an answer.

"That little bitch attacked me!" Debbie yelled, while lunging at me.

My father had full control of her as he grabbed her by the shoulders and shook the shit out of her. "She's a child Debbie!" He said shaking her so hard she looked like one of those bobble head dolls.

"Daddy she hit me!" I yelled waiting for my father to take me in his arms and cradle me as he always did. But he just stood there looking at me with sorrow in his eyes.

"Summer go home, you don't live here no more." He said almost whispering.

I grabbed hold of him tightly wrapping my arms around his waist.

"Daddy this is my home. I want to sleep in my bed, I want to sleep in my room. I don't want to live at Grandma's house anymore!" I screamed through tears.

I could see Debbie standing there with a smirk on her ugly wrinkled face. The bitch was still sporting Jheri curls, even though it was the nineties.

"Listen Summer, you a child, you too young to understand what's going on. I want you to go back home to your mama, and leave me with some peace." He said and with a little shove he ushered me out of the door and out of his life for good.